The

Invincible Refugees

THE HUGUENOT WEAVERS' HOUSE AT CANTERBURY

See page 123

The Invincible Refugees

The Story of the Huguenots

BETH COOMBE HARRIS

First printed by The Protestant Truth Society
Fleet Street, London

PROVIDENCE BOOKS
Millbank, Victoria Road, Windmill Hill, East Sussex BN27 4TG

CONTENTS

FOREWORD

AFTER perusing this engaging book, one is irresistably led to the great fundamental truth enunciated by the writer of the Epistle to the Hebrews in chapter thirteen, verse eight :—

> "*Jesus Christ is the same yesterday and to-day, yea and for ever*" (R.V.);

for this is the secret of the glorious record of stedfast adherence to the Protestant Faith exhibited by the Huguenots throughout their prolonged years of bitter persecution and suffering even unto death, and among whom this fascinating story is cast.

Miss Beth Coombe Harris maintains her artist faculty of throwing herself into the very midst of those whose lives she portrays; and—like the Prophet Ezekiel of old—"sits where the people sit." The period is that of the closing years of the seventeenth century; and the scene opens in the Normandy area of France, but—later—moves to the vicinity of Rye and Canterbury, where the Huguenot refugees found both welcome and hospitality.

Interest is aroused from the start and sustained throughout, by a chain of historically founded incidents depicting the relentless persecution of the Huguenots that started with the Massacre of Saint Bartholomew some hundred years previously, and was revived with terrific intensity by King Louis XIV and his bigoted advisers. A happier tone prevails as the principal characters reach the shelter of our own land, and throughout the narrative is the golden chain of the "one touch of nature that makes the whole world kin": but an outstanding feature is the number of instances in varied walks of life of people of all ages brought fully out from the fetters of Roman Catholicism by the simple presentation of the Gospel of the Grace of God, supported by the unflinching testimony and witness of many Huguenots who, under direst stress and pressure, cheerfully accepted heart-rending anguish and death rather than depart from their Protestant Faith.

Incidentally also, we are reminded how much we owe to-day to these French refugees; and learn the origin of bagpipes as well as how to culinarily utilise oxtails, and grow vegetables to healthful and profitable account. Nationally, this persecution cost France the loss of—it is estimated—well over a million valuable citizens and skilled artizans; whose exodus to England proved a corresponding asset of incalculable value, the results of which still exist in many far reaching ramifications.

All this—and more—is embodied in this excellent volume; which is cordially recommended in this our day, when the menace of Rome is revealing itself in so many and divers quarters and often unsuspected.

A. R. EMDIN.

Heathfield,
Sussex.

Chapter I

THE OLD HOME IN FRANCE

THE room was very quiet. The only sounds were the crackling of the logs in the closed stove, and the rustle of paper, as the man at the desk turned the pages of the note books, which lay in front of him.

A boy of fourteen sat at a table in the window, studying a book, his lips moved occasionally as he committed a lesson to memory.

Outside, in the stone-flagged courtyard, pigeons strutted to and fro, or flew in circles to alight again and peck at the corn which had been scattered for their supper. The breeze rustled the young leaves of a chestnut tree which grew in the walled garden beyond the courtyard, its boughs overhanging the wall. It was a peaceful spot at the back of Monsieur Durand's dwelling. The front faced a narrow street, noisy with the feet of many passers-by in their sabots, and the rattle of wheels on the cobbled thoroughfare. In the upper rooms of the house, for many hours daily, the clatter of looms could be heard, but now in the evening the looms were silent, the workpeople having returned to their homes.

M. Durand's face was grave as he studied his note books and made calculations on a sheet of paper. He had reason enough for gravity in the year of our Lord 1684, in the reign of the bigoted tyrant Louis XIV of France, for M. Durand was a Protestant, one of the large number of French people, hated and persecuted by the king.

Gaston Durand had just closed his books and pushed back his chair, when a slight scratch at the door intimated that someone without wished to come in. In response to M. Durand's " enter," a serving wench appeared and said, " The Pastor has come to see you Master."

" Ah ! That is welcome news," M. Durand responded. " Bring the Pastor hither."

The boy at the table rose and asked : " Shall I go Sir? "

" No, André, my son. I want you to hear what the Pastor and I have to discuss. It is necessary for you to know my plans and I know I can trust you. I have no need to warn you that the success of my arrangements depend a great deal on secrecy."

" Yes, you can trust me father," André said simply.

The father smiled, but a sigh followed immediately. Too well he knew that the children of the Huguenots learnt early to be careful how they talked. The terrible daily happenings in every village and town taught caution to young and old alike. The fear of the dragonnade * was no light matter.

The Pastor, an elderly man entered and after a cordial greeting to both André and his father, took a seat by the stove, spreading out his hands to catch the genial warmth, for although it was the month of May, the evening air was fresh and M. Fevré was frail and felt any change in the atmosphere more than many.

" Any news, Pastor ? " Gaston Durand inquired.

" No good news, my friend. Alas my poor flock, like helpless sheep, are harried by the fierce wolf. From petty annoyances, to the most exasperating cruelty, nothing is wanting on the part of the king and his abettors."

" Yes indeed that is so," M. Durand answered. " Have they not debarred all Huguenots from holding public offices. Huguenot teachers are only permitted to give instruction in reading, writing and arithmetic. We

---

* The persecution of French Protestants under Louis XIV by raids of dragoons (soldiers).

may only bury our dead at midnight, we may not sing at any of our meetings, many places of worship have been burnt, worst of all is the kidnapping of children and forcing them to become Roman Catholics. My wife is terribly nervous if André or his little sister is late from school. A lad of seven, who lived but a short distance from here, has been taken and made to sign a paper stating that he is a Roman Catholic. It appears to me that the king wishes to exasperate us into open rebellion, to give him an excuse for another massacre, as that of St. Bartholomew."

"That may be so, my friend. But have you heard that the king has taken alarm at the fact that so many Huguenots are disposing of their property and leaving the country, and has issued an edict forbidding any one to proceed abroad without express permission, any one disobeying this edict will suffer severe penalties?"

"Alas! I had not heard of that. In spite of the king, many will still leave. Our poor foolish king, he is losing the best of his subjects, the steady, the honest, the hard-working are going. Other countries will benefit. Trade must suffer. Thousands who have paid taxes will no longer be here. What evil genius prompts the king to such short sighted policy?"

'Madame de Maintenon is at the moment largely responsible for fresh outbursts of fury and cruelty on the king's part. Do you know her history?" the Pastor asked.

M. Durand replied in the negative.

"It is a sad story. She belonged to the D'Aubigny family, noted for their staunch Protestantism. The family possessed one Roman Catholic relative, this relation had the child forcibly removed to a convent, where for a time the girl held firm to the belief of her fathers, but her resistance weakened under persecution and inducement, and she turned Roman Catholic. She became an apt pupil of her instructors, and when she left the convent to become the wife of Scarron the wit and scoffer, she flung herself into the gay, social life of her husband's home. After his death she obtained the post of governess to some children at the court, where her beauty and wit attracted the attention of the king. She soon learnt to wield great influence over him, and found that as he hated the Huguenots she could please him by fanning the flame of his fury against her former co-religionists."

"Poor unhappy woman. What terrible responsibility is theirs, who poisoned that unfortunate child's mind against the true faith and made her what she is," M. Durand said.

"Yes, she is to be pitied. But my friend I came here to know what the plans are of which you gave me a hint a few days ago," the Pastor remarked.

Gaston Durand drew his chair close to his friend and spoke in a low tone.

"I feel, Pastor, that before things get still worse I must take my family to a place of safety where we can worship God without let or hindrance. I have been selling my property, at a great loss truly, but I have been more fortunate than some, who have gone off practically destitute. You know Pastor that my huge wagon goes laden with cloth to the coast every month, where a ship takes my merchandise to England and returns with the fleeces from that land, which my workpeople wash, card and weave into sayes, bayes and taffetas. Well, I propose when the time comes for the wagon to go again, to load the front as usual with the bales, but behind, my wife, my sister Marie and my little daughter Ninon will be concealed, as well as one of my looms which I must take to our destination, England, as a pattern for making more. There will also be a couple of sacks filled with louis d'or and food for the journey. Several of my workpeople intend following us and with God's blessing I hope to arrive safely in England and set up my looms there."

André was listening intently, and with great interest, he waited to hear what his father proposed for him and was glad to hear him say, "André has done the journey to the coast with me once already, so it will occasion no surprise if others see him riding on the front seat with me, or walking beside the horses."

Gaston Durand paused and the Pastor said earnestly but sadly : "God grant you a peaceful journey my friend. There are many perils, Louis' spies are everywhere, ready to arrest those who are seeking to leave our land."

"Yes, but in spite of this, thousands are getting away into Holland, Switzerland, Denmark, and Sweden, and some have gone as far as America. God's care is over them and in various disguises the escape is made. What about yourself Pastor ? Will you not come with us ? I am sure there will be room enough in the wagon for you."

The Pastor shook his head.

"Nay my friend. There are hundreds of my poor flock unable to escape and my place is with them. I have neither wife nor child, I value not my life if I can but comfort some in my charge. For you it is different. You have this dear lad on the threshold of life to consider, and your wife and daughter. Do not delay but go as soon as possible. Each day the danger increases."

"I am hastening my preparations, but I do not wish to reach Havre until the ship 'The Venture' is likely to be in port, that will not be for another fortnight, so I must not set out for a week. We shall travel as much as possible by night to avoid attracting attention. I know several places where we can hide by day. I have done the journey to the coast ever since my boyhood, so every yard of the road is familiar to me."

Gaston Durand paused, then turning to his son said: " My boy, it is past your bed time you must go now."

He put his hand on the lad's shoulder with an affectionate gesture and the Pastor said: " It is good for you, my friend, that you have a son growing old enough to enter into your plans and share the perils of your venture."

" Yes indeed. I know André will do his best to aid us all. Is that not so, my son? "

" Oh yes father. Thank you for telling me what you are planning." André replied.

André felt that he was leaving his boyhood days behind him, not that they had been care-free for long past. The trials of his parents and neighbours could not but make a difference even to a child's outlook. Now when he was to leave the home where he had dwelt all his life and go to a strange country, listen to a strange tongue, mix with a people of strange customs, André's feelings were somewhat conflicting, there was regret at what was to be left behind and yet an exhilarating desire for new scenes and fresh adventures mingled in the boy's mind and heart.

" Before André goes I would like to have a word of prayer with you," the Pastor said. " Is Madame Durand free to join us? "

" André go and find out and ask Aunt Marie to come also," M. Durand said. " We shall all value your prayers Pastor. My wife would have been here with us now, but little Ninon has a feverish attack and is restless, so my wife is with her."

André soon returned accompanied by his mother and aunt, both of whom greeted the Pastor cordially.

" Rachelle, my dear, the Pastor wishes to commend us to God, it may be for the last time, for he is going on a little tour of the villages to-morrow and we may be gone ere he returns," Gaston Durand explained to his wife.

All knelt and the Pastor poured out his heart in intercession. André never forgot that prayer as the Pastor commended each one to God. The words: "May this dear lad's life be for Thy glory, may he uphold the Light of the Gospel by lip and life, may he bring blessing to many lives, make him true to Thee and to Thy word," stirred André's heart greatly.

He had given his heart to the Lord two years previously, now as he knelt beside his mother the tears came into his eyes as he whispered: "O God make me what the Pastor is asking."

Chapter II

HUMBLE FOLK

THAT same evening in a humble dwelling in a narrow, back street, three of M. Durand's workpeople were busy completing their preparations for flight.

Jacques Goyer was M. Durand's foreman, a keen Huguenot, who up to then had steadily refused to pretend to be "converted" by his Papist neighbours. There were many, who, although truly Christian in heart, yet through the severity of the treatment received and the threats of worse to follow, abjured their religion. Numerous fathers and mothers, with the menace of having children taken from them and placed in Roman Catholic convents hanging over them, conformed outwardly to the will of the persecutors.

Jacques Goyer, his wife Colette and his daughter Jacqueline were engaged in putting together a few clothes and small possessions such as could be easily carried, for the time had come when it was impossible for them to remain any longer in their home in safety. They must flee speedily if they were to go at all. The guard on the frontier lines and the coast were becoming more rigid every day. Already hundreds had left the neighbourhood, some alas! to be captured and brought back loaded with chains and then thrown into dungeons or sent to the galleys for life.

Jacques Goyer's face was set with quiet determination, his wife now and again tried to make some cheering remark, although her heart ached as she looked around on the simple but beloved home, with its household possessions, which she must now leave never to see again.

The shining copper pots, the old oak chest with brass hinges, the mugs and plates that Colette had prized and cared for with housewifely skill must all be left, but she knew that if she had her husband and daughter still with her, these other things were comparatively of small importance.

The saddest of the three was apparently Jacqueline, a slight pretty girl of seventeen. Her tears dropped as she did her mother's bidding, although her parents noticed her grief they made no comment, for they knew the cause and felt no words of theirs could help.

A footstep on the path outside made them start and begin to hurriedly hide away their bundles, and try to look as though nothing out of the usual was happening. But a low voice at the hole in the door, where the string attached to the bobbin hung, re-assured them.

"It is only Pierre."

Jacques Goyer hastened to open the door and a stalwart young man stepped in.

"Then you are really going," he said after greeting each member of the family.

"Yes, my lad. We have no choice in the matter. I only wish it were possible for you to come with us, but I know I must not tempt you. Your duty is here."

"How is your mother to-night?" Colette asked.

"Sadly, sadly," Pierre answered. Then with a look at Jacqueline he continued: "She would like to see Jacqueline once more, if you will allow me to take her home this evening."

Jacqueline's face was eager. It was the last chance of a walk with her lover, but although her eyes were eloquent, her lips were silent. Parental authority was strong in those days and had Jacqueline's parents refused their permission, Jacqueline would have said nothing, but her tears would have fallen again, for the moment she had ceased crying.

Jacqueline's mother spoke quickly, turning to her husband she said :" 'Tis but seven o'clock father. Don't you think Jacqueline could go just for an hour ? 'Tis but a short walk."

Jacques frowned. The streets were full of danger, but not more or greater than Jacqueline would have to face in their flight.

" I will take care of her and bring her back," Pierre said eagerly, and Jacqueline's father consented saying however : " I will fetch her in a half hour's time. She must be safely indoors before eight."

Jacqueline quickly donned cloak and hood and the two started.

For a moment or two they were silent. Hearts were too full for ready speech. Presently Jacqueline said : " If only you could come too Pierre. Shall we ever meet again? "

Pierre's voice was gruff with emotion. " God grant we may. I know I am doing my duty by staying with my old mother. She has the spirit to go but not the strength. That stroke she had paralysed her legs. Try to be cheerful with her dearest. I make light to her of the perils that surround us, yet I know that any day I might be hauled off to the galleys."

Jacqueline shivered. That fear was ever in her heart but to hear it put into words made it seem more imminent.

The two soon reached the little home where Pierre and his mother lived. It was surrounded by a small garden and here in its seclusion they stood. Pierre took Jacqueline in his arms whispering : " My love, my own love, be true to me, and some day I will join you in England. I will find you, no matter where you are. Never fear. God keep you, my dear heart. Every moment my thoughts will be with you and my prayers ascend for you."

Jacqueline clung to him saying brokenly : " I will be true to you Pierre. There will never be anyone like you. I never remember the time when you weren't my dearest love. Surely God has brought us together and He will help us."

" Yes, yes. Our trust is in Him. God make you brave my dearest."

Fain would the two have lingered there in that sweet, sad embrace, but Jacqueline remembered that time was flying and Pierre's mother must not be disappointed.

" Come Pierre, I must see your mother a few moments before father comes," she said.

So together they entered the cottage and the old woman's face brightened at their approach. The depth of Pierre's unselfishness could be measured by the fact that he had succeeded in keeping his mother in ignorance of his desire to accompany Jacqueline and her parents in their flight. His sacrifice was made cheerfully and the ache of his heart was hidden. Althought Pierre's mother was almost helpless, her mental faculties were unimpaired and she took the opportunity of this brief visit to ask many questions. She wanted to know all about the Goyers' plans and Jacqueline told her.

" You remember hearing of that old pedlar whom we sheltered a few months back, and who died with us. Well, father is going to wear his clothes and take his stock and go as a pedlar. M. Fontaine at the farm is selling us a donkey and panniers. Some of our things will be packed in the panniers and just the top layer will be things to sell. I am to go with father as his boy. I don't like having to cut my hair off—"

Pierre exclaimed, for Jacqueline's hair was beautiful. A copper brown glinting with gold, fine in texture and yet abundant.

The old woman smiled and said : " Never mind it will soon grow again. When you come back to France as

I'll be bound you will when these little troubles have blown over, it will be as nice as ever."

"I mustn't think of trifles like losing my hair and having my face stained to look as though I had been exposed to the sun and air. That is nothing in comparison to what others are suffering."

"And your mother, Jacqueline, how is she going?"

"Mother is going to come along behind us, as if she were alone. She is to wear ragged garments and will carry a bundle of firewood on her head. We hope to be able to lodge at the same inns at night, or shelter together in the woods, but mother is very brave and says she'll manage all right even if she has to be alone."

Jacqueline spoke so calmly that no one would have guessed how sad and tremulous her heart was, but self-control had been learnt in a hard school, and she was a worthy daughter of her courageous parents.

"What part are you making for?" was the next question.

"Holland," Jacqueline answered. "We hope to get to England from there. Father wants to join his master M. Durand in England, but the ships are being so closely watched now it is easier to slip over the frontier and get into Holland."

"It's a big undertaking, my dear. I fancy you'd all do better to stay here and hope for happier days. That's what my Pierre thinks, isn't it Pierre."

The invalid knew little of the suffering of the Protestants, she thought it only amounted to a few inconveniences, and her son was anxious that she should remain in this blissful ignorance.

Pierre would have found it difficult to reply to this remark, but he was saved from the necessity by the arrival of Jacqueline's father. He came in and sat down for a short chat with the old woman. Pierre and Jacqueline took the opportunity of leaving the sick room.

In the little kitchen they clung to each other, their young hearts wrung with anguish, the future so uncertain and dark, Jacqueline's tears flowed afresh and Pierre's eyes were not without moisture.

"Promise, promise again Jacqueline that no one shall take my place," Pierre whispered.

"I do promise, with all my heart I promise, Pierre," Jacqueline replied.

"Be brave, my little one. I shall come to you. It may be years hence, but I shall come. I have the assurance in my heart that it will be so. You will see your Pierre walking in wherever you are."

Before Jacqueline could make reply her father's voice was heard.

"Come my child. 'Tis terribly late, nigh curfew time I feel certain."

Jacques Goyer's tone was gruff. It hurt him to see his daughter's tears, but the parting must come and it was useless to delay.

So a hasty farewell was said and Jacques Goyer and Jacqueline wended their way home.

CHAPTER III

THE SOLDIER'S WARNING

RACHELLE DURAND was restless. André should have been back from school a half-an-hour before then. She stood at the front door of the house looking up and down the street, then she returned to the living room and put some finishing touches to the meal set on the big table, assuring herself while she did so, that André had only lingered playing with some school fellows and making up her mind to take him to task for this, as he knew how anxious she always was, if he or Ninon were late home from school. Ninon had not been to school that day for she was only just beginning to get over her feverish attack, so Madame Durand had no concern about her.

Aunt Marie came downstairs and into the room at that moment. She at once noticed the look of anxiety on her sister-in-law's face and asked: "What is worrying you dear?"

"André has not returned from school," Rachelle replied briefly.

"Dear, dear! May be he has been kept in for some little fault." Marie suggested hoping to allay her sister-in-law's fears.

"I hope that may be so—but you understand my alarm."

Marie understood only too well. She shivered at the thought implied by Rachelle's words.

André, bonny bright André. If he should be caught and dragged off to some monastery, what would be their anguish? And yet there were many who were suffering thus. The two women went to the door, Rachelle going a few steps up the road to a turning where she could have a longer view. Her husband was approaching, but no André.

Rachelle turned back. Her face growing whiter still.

However her colour returned in a few moments, as André's whistle was heard and in he came with a rush, flinging his arms around his mother in an embrace.

"My son, why have you given me this anxiety? Why did you linger on your homeward way?" Madame Durand asked.

"Mother you will understand when I explain. Here comes father let me tell you together. Just when I was passing the bridge with some of the boys on my way home, * the soldier on sentinel duty called to us, 'For pity sake get me a drink of water. I am faint but I dare not leave my post.' The other boys laughed at him, but Mother, I knew you and father would not have wished me to ignore his need, so I told him I would get him some water. 'Twas a long way to a pump and then I had to borrow a mug from a house near by, in which to carry the water and go back to the bridge. The soldier was grateful and made me tell him my name and address. He drank like any one desperate. After that I had to go back to the people who had lent me the mug. So that's why I'm late. Whew! I'm hot, I simply ran all the way home. I hope you do not think I did wrong, Sir," André said turning to his father.

"No my boy. I would never wish you to be callous to any one's need," Gaston Durand answered.

"Gaston, you do not think this might be a trap, a ruse for getting André's name and address?" Rachelle said.

"Dear heart, you see danger in everything. André, did the man look ill?"

* A true incident.

"Oh yes indeed Sir. He looked ghastly. I really think he needed the water."

"Well, come, supper is ready. I am glad to have you safely indoors, André," Madame Durand said.

Little eight-year-old Ninon was well enough to join the family, and for her sake there was no mention of the impending departure, the thought of which filled the minds of the others.

That evening Gaston Durand told his wife that he considered they must make their start in four days' time, to reach Havre at the right moment when the ship would be ready for his merchandise.

Rachelle assured her husband that the supply of food would be ready, in fact it was ready, save for the packing.

"We must take this with us," she said placing her hand on a huge bulky volume which lay on a table.

"Ah ! yes, most certainly," Gaston replied.

The book in question was a Bible, which had been a treasured possession in the Durand family for over a hundred years. It had been printed in Antwerp in the year 1529, by a printer named Jacques le Fevre, originally in separate portions, now bound together and covered with leather. The leather was scorched and showed signs of having been in or near a fire. André and Ninon were never tired of hearing the story of the Bible and how it had been saved from destruction. Their father's great-grandfather was the first owner of the Book and after he had possessed it a few years, it, and every other copy of the Scriptures in the neighbourhood, had been seized by the priests, with the object of destroying them by fire. A huge fire was made in the market place and book after book flung in. The flames were fierce and the men doing the wicked act could not get near. One hefty priest flung M. Durand's Bible with such a powerful aim that it whirled through the flames and fell, only scorched, across the bonfire. A woman, who had a stall there in the market place, saw what had happened and as every one else was standing facing the fire, she had the opportunity of picking up the Bible and hiding it behind her stall. Her one idea was to make a little money by selling it to some one, and finding M. Durand's name in the volume, she took it to him hidden in her market basket under a cloth. M. Durand gladly rewarded her for returning it to him. Now it was Gaston Durand's greatest treasure, read daily, from it he and his wife derived comfort in their difficult circumstances, strength to endure and hope for the future.

Together Gaston and Rachelle discussed their plans and preparations and presently retired to rest.

The next day passed quietly until the family was gathered at the evening meal, when a knock came at the door. The serving maid rose from her seat at the lower end of the table and went to see who was there. She quickly returned looking somewhat alarmed.

'Tis a soldier, Master! " she said.

A soldier ! What did that portend ? Rachelle Durand turned pale but she spoke calmly.

" Gaston you will interview the man."

Her husband already moving from his chair. He went out of the room closing the door behind him. In a few minutes he came back saying: " André, it is the man you befriended yesterday, he wishes to speak to you privately. I have put him in the study."

André went with alacrity to see what the soldier wanted.

" How are you now ? he asked. " I hope all right to-day."

" Young Sir, I have only a few moments to spare, but I owe you a kindness, for you helped me yesterday. I have just heard that twenty-five soldiers are to be quartered in your household to-morrow. I do not know what your father can do, but it struck me it might help him if he were warned. I must not linger. I have to be on duty in ten minutes time. Keep it secret that I have told you this."

André was almost speechless with horror. He could only murmur: "Thank you, thank you," as he held the door open for the man to leave.

Returning to the family, André said quietly: "Father can I have speech with you. I have something important to tell you."

M. Durand immediately left the room with his son and André briefly told the news. His father passed his hand over his face with a gesture of dismay, but he quickly recovered himself and said: "André we must leave here to-night. With twenty-five soldiers quartered on us, escape would be impossible and I would not have your mother and aunt exposed for a moment to their ribaldry and insults. This means that we are suspected of making plans to leave our land and it is to make that action impossible that the soldiers are coming. Thank God that you were able to help that man yesterday and so have been the instrument in God's Hand to aid our flight. Ask your mother to come hither."

Rachelle Durand exclaimed in horror when she heard her husband's story.

"Twenty-five soldiers, Gaston! But by law a house of this size is only obliged to take twelve."

"Yes dear, but I heard only yesterday that the king's minister, Louvois has written to the head of our district, saying that a great number of horsemen and officers are to be billeted on Protestants, if according to just distribution ten would be quartered, we are to be ordered to take twenty. But we will not stay to discuss this. We must be off to night, as soon as it is dark. I hope by travelling until dawn, we shall reach the farm of my friend Daniel Morel, where we can hide and rest before starting on another stage of our journey. We must pack everything into the wagon at once. Fortunately our courtyard is secluded, so if we work quietly no one will know what we are doing."

There was no time for regrets or commiseration. Madame Durand's first act was to send her serving maid to her home telling her she need not return until the morning. The maid was fond of her mistress and probably could be trusted, but she was a Catholic, and Rachelle Durand was running no risks. Then she and Aunt Marie set to work packing the food, while M. Durand and André arranged the wagon.

Everything went on successfully and by dark, Rachelle Durand, Aunt Marie and Ninon were tucked in at the back of the wagon, while André took his place on the front seat and Gaston Durand led the horses out of the yard. So the start was made.

Chapter IV

MADAME FURNEAUX

EARLIER on that same day, in a chateau some six or seven miles away from Gaston Durand's dwelling, a lady sat in her boudoir, reading a letter. It was from her husband who had gone away from home ostensibly on business, but in reality to seek a suitable refuge in Switzerland for himself, his wife and child.

Madame Furneaux was a sincere, Huguenot Christian and was well known in the neighbourhood as such. Her life was spent in caring for the poor, the aged and sick in the village near her home. Her husband was nominally a Huguenot also, had there been no religious persecution, he would always have kept up his profession, but it did not seem worth while to him to suffer the loss of all things, for, what to him was, merely a creed. However he had great respect for his wife and a deep love for her and his child and to save Madame from persecution he had determined to take her, little Leonie and many members of his household to Geneva.

He had been gone a couple of weeks and Madame Furneaux was delighted to get the letter from him which she was now reading. The bearer of the letter, a faithful servant who had accompanied M. Furneaux on his travels, was now relating his experiences of the journey in the kitchen.

After a loving greeting to his wife M. Furneaux wrote: "I have found a lofty house under the shadow of the Cathedral of St. Pierre which we can rent for a time while I look for a dwelling more suitable for my darling wife and little daughter. I cannot wait to obtain that before fetching you, for I am only existing without you dearest, it is not life when I am separated from my wife. Besides I fear the threatened persecution may come to a head sooner than we at first anticipated and I long to know, dear heart, that you and Leonie are safe. There is always the danger of a child being wrested from its Huguenot parents and placed in a convent and if that happened your heart, not to say anything of mine, would be broken. I suppose it is useless, my love, to suggest that you should conform outwardly to the authorities, many are doing so. The king's minister Louvois professes to have made sixty thousand conversions in a short time in Bordeaux. When the soldiers are billeted on Huguenot families, to avoid the awful insults to which they are subjected, some give in. It appears to me that, under the circumstances, you would be justified in conforming, of course still holding your own views in your heart, however I would not coerce you, I merely make the suggestion because I long to know you are safe."

Madame Furneaux put down the letter and tears filled her eyes.

"My poor husband, I wish that the love of God was stronger in his heart," she murmured.

She sat a few moments pondering, then took up the letter again and continued reading.

"But that is enough about that. You will soon be here in safety I hope, and at liberty to hold what views you please. Expect me to arrive soon after this letter reaches you. I have only to wait to sign an agreement for the house and to get some furniture together as I fear we can bring none with us. Our departure must take place as unostentatiously as possible. I must try to sell our estate through an agent, but it will grieve me to let our old chateau, which has been in my family for hundreds of years, pass into the hands of a stranger, but that matters little as long as I have you. This is a lovely spot, the snowy swans swim majestically on the blue waters of the lake, there are charming walks and I think you will be happy here. Now I must bring this epistle to a close only adding my love to you, my dearest wife, whom I hope to embrace shortly."

To this was added a postscript: "Since writing the above I have heard of a chateau at Estavover which I think I can purchase. It is on the lake Neuchatel, a wonderful stretch of water which I visited some years ago. I remember the colour of the lake was constantly changing, white at dawn, becoming blue later, deepening in tone as the day advances and reflecting rosy tints at sunset. In bad weather it darkens, but is ever varying and is . . . . ."

Madame Furneaux put down the letter abruptly, for the sound of the clatter of horses' feet reached her ears. She rushed to the window, her cheeks flushing with pleasure as she thought: "My husband has come."

But her face paled with horror a moment later, for not her husband rode over the drawbridge, but an officer of the king, followed by a band of soldiers.

"The dragonnade," she murmured. "God keep me true to Him."

She heard the officer demanding an interview with Madame Furneaux, evidently they knew her husband was away. Bravely with apparent calmness, although her heart was throbbing painfully, she descended the broad staircase and as the officer, closely followed by his men, entered the hall she confronted him.

The man bowed low with feigned politeness.

"Madame, it is your king's wish that I and my men shall be billeted here."

"The chateau is at your disposal, sir. I only ask that my own apartment and my child's nursery may not be invaded."

Again the man bowed low.

"It is your king's pleasure that I shall ask you a question. Will you attend mass to-morrow morning and publicly signify your willingness to embrace the faith of your king?"

"Sir, the commands of my Lord and Saviour Jesus Christ are more to me than the command of the king. Permit me to ask you a question. When you come to the day of your death will you be ready to meet God? How will you give an account to Him of the way you are treating His children? We are precious to Him . . ."

The officer's face was a study. Amazement for a moment seemed to paralyse him, that a woman should have the courage to speak to him thus, when she knew that her life was in peril, was too astounding for words, but with an effort and an oath he pulled himself together. It was useless to waste time on argument. Madame Furneaux was known as an obstinate heretic, the sooner she was dealt with the better. He jerked his hand over his shoulder saying one word: "fire."

A moment later Madame Furneaux fell to the ground, riddled with bullets. Death was instantaneous and she was spared the suffering that many of her compatriots endured.

No sooner had Madame fallen than the soldiers rushed through the castle terrifying the servants, some of whom purchased their lives by abjuring their faith, while others, refusing to conform, were ruthlessly slain.

Little Leonie's nurse, Marthé, hearing the shouting and sound of firing ran to the head of the staircase, Leonie following her closely, and looking down, the nurse saw what had happened. Her loved mistress lay in a pool of blood, her white face upturned. With a gasp of horror, Marthé caught up Leonie who was exclaiming: "Maman, Maman." Carrying the child in her arms, Marthé ran down a back staircase and hence into the grounds, seeking to make her escape.

She had just reached the road when a soldier espied her and followed. Marthé heard his footsteps on the road and she hastily hid Leonie behind a shrub saying: " Stay there darling," she then turned back to meet the man, her one thought being to distract his attention from her little charge. The soldier lifted his musketoon with the intention of firing, but seeing that his victim was a young and pretty girl, he changed his mind and dragged her back into the house.

Poor girl ! had swift death been her portion it would indeed have been merciful. Brought before the officer and given the chance of recanting she bravely refused.

" Will you die for a creed ? " asked the man.

" No sir, but for love to my Saviour I would die rather than deny Him," Marthé replied.

Delivered over to the brutality of the soldiers, Marthé passed hours of horror, until at last one man more compassionate than the others shot her and her body was flung into the moat. One of the thousands of French martyrs who loved not their lives unto the death, accepting suffering rather than escape through denial of their Lord.

Meanwhile little Leonie getting tired of sitting behind the bush where her nurse had placed her, ran out into the road crying: " Nurse, nurse." Tears were streaming down her face as she ran on and on, mercifully away from her home, until, at last, worn out she sank down on a grassy verge by the side of the road and fell asleep, not awaking until the early dawn.

Chapter V

ANDRE'S DISCOVERY

THE hours of the night passed slowly and anxiously to Gaston Durand, as he trudged beside his horses drawing the wagon which sheltered his dearest possessions.

André had kept his father company for a time, until his father, noticing the weary droop of the boy's figure, had insisted on his joining his mother, aunt and sister in the wagon, where he soon fell asleep. Ninon slept also, but the two women, Rachelle and Marie, kept vigil. Occasionally they spoke to each other in whispers, but for the most part they were silent, busy with their thoughts. Rachelle's eyes filled with tears now and again, although she hastily brushed them away, determined not to distress her dear ones by weeping. But she had always been a home-lover, supremely happy in caring for her husband and children, keeping her house in spotless order, guiding her maidservant and seeking to make every one under her roof happy. Now she must turn back on the dear, sweet days and go forth to a strange land, to find a new home among unknown people.

Memory was busy and she visualised the home she had left, and which she would probably never see again. How dear it was to her, it always had been, and now was doubly so in this moment of departure. The big rooms, the old oak beams, the high gables and inglenook, she seemed to see them all. The broad courtyard, where the pigeons strutted on the cobble stones, the door in the massive stone wall which surrounded three sides of the courtyard, opening into a garden, a garden which although more strictly meant for use than pleasure, was nevertheless an endless source of enjoyment to the good housewife. How she had loved in the early morning gathering the herbs for the *pot-au-feu.* What would it be like in that strange England where scarce a vegetable could be obtained? She had heard that neither cabbage, carrots nor celery grew there. Such a condition of affairs seemed the acme of desolation to the thrifty housewife.

So far had she got in her thoughts, when the stirring of Ninon in her sleep, checked her. She said to herself: "What a wicked woman I am; so full of doubts and fears, why I should be praising God that we are all together and so far on our journey. If André had not befriended that poor soldier, we should have had no warning of the dragoons being billeted on us, and then when once they had arrived, there would have been no opportunity of escape. Those terrible men whom the king calls 'His booted missionaries.'"

"Yes indeed she had much to be thankful for and God Who had helped them so far would be their Refuge and Aid in the unknown future."

As if to confirm her thoughts, her sister-in-law Marie put her hand on Rachelle's arm and whispered: "Do not be downhearted dear, God is with us. He knows our need and He Who was a wall of fire protecting the Children of Israel from the Egyptians is still the same to-day."

"Ah Marie, I wish I had your faith," Rachelle replied.

And so the dark hours of the night passed. Just at dawn, André awoke with a start and exclaimed: "Oh I've slept and let father do all the watching!"

His tone was so reproachful and dismayed, that his mother smiled: "Father was glad for you to get a good sleep, my son."

André soon sprang out of the wagon and walked with

his father. The eastern sky was beginning to lighten, birds were awaking in the hedges and singing their morning song of praise, all nature seemed at peace, but the hearts of men and women all over the fair land of France were torn with anxiety and fear.

Presently André paused and said: " What was that father? It sounded like the cry of a little child."

" Nay, my son. It was but the cry of a trapped animal, a rabbit or a hare I expect. Their cries are often somewhat like that of a child."

But the cry came again and again, and Gaston hesitated. It did sound like a child in distress.

" Listen André ! We shall reach the top of this hill in about five mintes, the horses are bound to go slowly till then, for they are tired and the load is heavy. On the turn of the hill we must hasten. I want to reach the farm before people are astir, we then can hide there to-day and start afresh at dusk. You are fleet of foot, you can run down that lane from which the cry comes, see what is wrong and still be at the top of the hill as soon as the horses. But don't linger, it will endanger all our lives if we have to wait for you. Remember I trust you, André."

" I will remember Sir," André said and darted off down the lane that ran at a right angle from the road on which they were travelling.

He had gone but a few yards when he saw a little figure running towards him. It was Leonie. The child was crying bitterly, calling as she ran: " Nurse, nurse."

André quickly reached her and taking her in his arms sought to comfort her.

" Don't cry dear," he said. " André will take care of you."

She put her little arms round his neck pressing her tear-stained face against his cheek and soon she stopped sobbing as she said: " Dear, dear boy."

André was a kind-hearted boy, with a natural instinct to protect the helpless, now it stirred in his heart in a stronger way than ever before. He could not have put his thoughts into words, but a strange sense of strength filled him and a determination to care for and cherish this little one at all costs.

Reaching the wagon, he called excitedly: " Father, look ! "

Gaston Durand did look and instantly a thought of dismay came to him. What was he to do ? He dare not delay to hunt for the parents and home of this child. Were they to take her on with them ? It was the only thing to do. Perhaps at his friend's farm they could leave her, while inquiries were made. At the moment, speed was important, for it was rapidly getting light and there was the danger of meeting curious people or even enemies.

" Give her to your mother, André," M. Gaston said and André climbed into the wagon saying: " Look mother, I have found this little girl wandering all alone."

Rachelle and Marie Durand felt as dismayed as Gaston had done, but the foremost instinct of them both was to care for the child.

Her clothes were soaked in dew and Madame Durand took her frock and underclothing off, while Marie opened a basket and got out some of Ninon's garments.

Ninon was now awake and said crossly: " That's my frock, she can't have that."

" But darling you would give your frock to this poor little girl who is so wet, wouldn't you ? "

Ninon pouted and did not reply, her mother took no further notice of her little daughter and proceeded to dry Leonie's hair and put on the frock. She noted the daintiness of the child's clothing and drew Marie's attention to a locket hanging to a thin gold chain round the little one's neck.

Tell me dear, what is your name?" Rachelle Durand asked.

"Leonie," the child answered adding a surname the pronunciation of which was indistinct, although most of her words were clear. She was able to tell them she was four years old and added of her own accord: "Big soldier caught nurse and dragged her away."

"And where was your mother, dear?" Marie asked.

The child began to cry and said between her sobs: "Maman lying on the floor, nasty blood all round her."

It seemed quite clear to the two women that there had been a dragonnade and the child's people had been killed. The best thing they could do was to draw the little one's attention to other matters. Marie suggested that no doubt she was hungry and such proved to be the case. A big slice of cake was eagerly welcomed and quickly devoured, Leonie nestling in Madame Durand's arms while she ate.

Meanwhile André was again walking beside his father. He asked: "Father why do you want to travel by night and hide by day. We have done this journey before openly and I do not see why anyone should be suspicious of us now, no one is to know that our intentions are to go to England. It looks just like the ordinary journey to the coast."

"Ah, but André the king's soldiers are everywhere hunting for Huguenots. If we meet a troop they would certainly search our wagon and the presence of our womenfolk would betray us at once. It would mean a convent for your mother and aunt, maybe worse than that, the galleys for me or death, and possibly the galleys for you. Boys of your age have been sent to the galleys for life. I shall be glad when we are hidden at the farm."

It was broad daylight now and Gaston urged the horses on.

"Just round that corner, André," he said, pointing with his whip.

"Soon be there, mother," he continued, turning his face toward the wagon.

But when they rounded the corner both André and his father exclaimed. The once peaceful, prosperous looking farmhouse was no more, blackened walls stood in its place, telling a silent tale of what had happened. The soldiers had been there and the Protestant family martyred. A big barn at a short distance was still standing, and Gaston Durand guided his horses thither, feeling too sorrowful for words.

An old man peeped cautiously out, and then seeing who was coming, advanced.

"Ah M. Durand, you come on a sad day. My poor master and mistress and their son all gone. I only escaped, for I hid in the loft among the hay. Alas! Alas! We live in terrible days. I suppose you are on your way to the coast."

"I am indeed grieved to hear your news, Simon. No one is safe in our land and because of this I am, as you guess, on my way to the coast, but not alone. I am taking my family to England. My wife, sister and children are in the wagon. I want to hide here to-day."

"Yes, yes, Monsieur. There is room in the barn and plenty of hay to rest in. The soldiers will not come back, for they think they have done their work well. It was a good thing for you that you did not arrive here yesterday."

The little party in the wagon were only too glad to alight, and entering the barn Rachelle Durand unpacked some food, while her husband and old Simon cared for the horses. Presently the old man came into the barn and his eye fell on Leonie, now seated contently beside André on a heap of hay.

"Why, who have you here, Madame? It is uncommonly like little Mademoiselle Furneaux from the chateau. Although I haven't seen the child for more than twelve months, I believe 'tis her. Her nurse was a friend of my mistress here and used to sometimes bring the little one to the farm."

Rachelle Durand explained how André had found the child wandering and added: " Perhaps you can suggest a way by which we can return her to her parents."

" Ah woe is the day ! " the old man said. " A lad from the chateau came this way last night, fleeing to his parents who live about two miles from here. He told me the soldiers had been at their foul work and the folks in the chateau were all killed, for they were Huguenots."

" Then we will keep the child and take her with us to England," Madame Durand said. " I feared something like that had happened, from the little the child told us."

Simon did not know, for the boy in his haste to get to his parents, had not said that M. Furneaux was in Switzerland, so the old man concluded that both of Leonie's parents were among the slain.

CHAPTER VI

THE JOURNEY

GASTON DURAND decided to linger two days in the shelter of the barn. He did not wish to reach the coast before the ship was due to arrive from England. He feared it would be a difficult matter to hide his family at Havre, where he understood the king's soldiers were keeping a sharp look out to arrest all Huguenots trying to escape. Every step was fraught with peril and Gaston could only look up to the Heavenly Father for guidance and wisdom for himself in his responsibility. He knew that if the good ship " The Venture " were in port, he could depend on help from the English captain, so it was advisable to delay reaching the coast until the right moment.

Entering the barn after caring for the horses, Gaston stood a moment contemplating his family. Strong man as he was and in the prime of life, yet the sad circumstances through which he was passing, the anxiety he felt for his dear ones, the night without sleep, all combined to give him a sense of exhaustion. His wife quickly noted his fatigue, and pulling some hay together to form a seat, she said: " Sit down Gaston and rest. After you have eaten you must sleep. I will watch while you slumber, for I had no exertion all night, even if I did not sleep much."

Placing some food before her husband, Rachelle coaxed him to eat, sitting beside him and making cheerful remarks.

" We've got each other dear heart, and nothing matters in comparison with that."

Gaston raised himself and put his arm around her.

"True dearest. We have much to be thankful for. Why you'd make a home of a bundle of hay and a few boughs under a hedge, where *you* are that is home to me. I feel refreshed now and shall be quite myself after a sleep. I think we had better stay here a couple of days, dear, then we must go forward, hiding in the woods by day and travelling by night."

He was a little dubious at first, when his wife said they must include Leonie in their party, but when Rachelle said: "What else can we do Gaston? We cannot desert a poor helpless child," he agreed and not many hours passed before Leonie had won all their hearts, with the exception of Ninon. Rachelle Durand had not realised that her little daughter possessed that peace destroying quality in her character, jealousy. There had been no occasion for Ninon to exhibit it in the eight years of her life, before this. Had she not been the pet of the household, with no small brother or sister to dispute her ownership of toys or good things? For André being six years older had no desire for Ninon's puppets or other childish possessions.

André was inclined to be indignant when Ninon protested at Leonie sitting on his mother's lap.

"Maman," Ninon said, "I am your little daughter, Leonie is not."

Rachelle Durand was wise. She answered the little pouting girl; "Of course you are my own dear little daughter, but this little girl has no mother, so we must be very kind to her. You will be a big sister to her won't you?"

The thought of being a big sister intrigued Ninon and she answered graciously: "Yes, she can be my little sister," adding a moment later: "She'll have to do just what I tell her."

Madame Durand did not argue the point. Later she

had a talk with André and told him that he should be very sorry for Ninon.

"You know André, if Ninon were lame or blind you would be sorry for her, well, this jealous disposition is a greater misfortune than a physical infirmity and we must help Ninon to overcome it. I am not sorry that circumstances have arisen that make this fault of hers evident, for I have great hopes that she will learn to conquer it while she is young."

"If Ninon loves Jesus and wants to please Him, she won't give way to it, mother," André said, and his mother agreed with him.

The days and nights of their travels passed, and Gaston Durand was thankful when they drew near to the end of their journey without being molested, and yet in spite of the mercies they had experienced so far, he could not but be anxious, as the most difficult part of the undertaking lay in front, that of getting the party on to the ship without being detected.

The last day they found a hiding place in the woods, and Gaston decided to go on to Havre on foot alone, for they were only about two miles from that port. He would then find out if "The Venture" had arrived and take counsel with Captain Hopkins.

Rachelle's heart sank within her when her husband told her what he was going to do. To be left without him for even a few hours, made her nervous, but she reminded herself that God was still watching over her, and nothing could befall unless it was His Will, and then grace would be given as it was needed. So she assumed a cheerful air as Gaston bade her "Goodbye," and returned to the wagon spending the hours of her husband's absence in keeping Ninon and Leonie happy and quiet. It was not an easy task, for the children slept all night while they were travelling, and each morning found them full of life and activity and they did not enjoy being kept in the wagon and talking only in hushed whispers.

Rachelle Durand was afraid of some stray pedestrian hearing any sound and discovering their hiding place.

Meanwhile Gaston Durand was delighted to find " The Venture " in port and Captain Hopkins standing on the little jetty. He greeted Gaston heartily and asked how soon the merchandise could be placed on board the ship. He was anxious to take advantage of a favourable wind and set sail.

Gaston took him aside to a quiet nook and then in low tones explained how matters stood.

Captain Hopkins gave a low whistle.

" Well Sir, I'm your man. I took two ladies and three men to England on my last voyage, a little party of Huguenots. They were of one family but had travelled in two parties not to attract attention. I tell you Sir, I nearly wept when I saw the ladies, they had travelled thirty leagues on foot along broken roads and almost trackless paths, enduring cold and hunger, disguised as peasants and were ill with fatigue. But there they are safe in England at last. Now what about your party? The best thing will be for you to bring them here on foot after dark. My men will have a boat ready at the jetty and will take them to the ship, where they can hide in the hold. To-morrow morning you can bring your wagon here and we will load up the merchandise. That will be nothing unusual, and you can go on board with your goods. But what about your wagon and horses? "

" I shall be obliged to leave them. I see no way of disposing of them. I must leave them at the inn and when I do not return for them, the innkeeper will draw his own conclusions and benefit by my loss."

" Not so fast, friend. I know a man living at a farm about a mile out. He is without religion but he hates this persecution and has lent a hand to many a fugitive. ' I'll slip out to his place and make a bargain with him, while you return to your family. You'll have to sell cheap, I fear, but that will be better than getting nothing. We can leave the wagon and horses at the inn as you said, but he can fetch them from there later."

"Thank you Captain. You are a good friend. May the Lord reward you for all you are doing for His children."

Captain Hopkins blew his nose noisily and exclaimed: "Tut, tut, man I want no reward, but you can say a prayer for me now and again. I'm a Protestant right enough, but I am afraid my religion isn't what it ought to be. Now, my old mother was a saint and many a prayer she offered for her boy, but there we must not stay here talking. You get back to your folk and be here at twelve o'clock to-night. The boat shall be waiting and the jetty will be deserted at that hour."

The little party in the woods were delighted when they heard M. Durand's signal that he was returning. The hoot of an owl three times in succession was his sign. They all greeted him eagerly.

"Is all right father?" André asked.

"Is the ship there?" Madame Durand queried.

While Aunt Marie wanted to know: "What plans have you made for us?"

Gaston Durand smiled as all these questions were fired at him.

"All in good time," he answered and then told them how they were to go into the town on foot after dark and by boat out to the ship.

It was the most perilous part of the journey and it was not to be wondered at that they felt grave. Towards evening they sat down to a meal, M. Durand pointing out to them that they would need strength for their undertaking and all must eat well. Next they knelt together in prayer, thanking God for His protecting care so far, and asking that He would guard and shelter them every step of the way. Finally they set out, M. Durand walking in front carrying Leonie and also a lantern. Madame Durand followed leading Ninon, Aunt Marie and André in the rear. The two little girls had been cautioned not to speak and both seemed to understand the situation. Little Leonie was exceedingly intelligent and said: " Nasty, bad soldier might get Leonie if she makes a noise."

To find the path out of the wood by night was not easy and although Gaston Durand thought he knew the way, yet he took a wrong track and after walking about twenty minutes they found themselves back at the wagon.

They all exclaimed, for the disappointment was great.

" Stand still a moment, " Gaston said, " we must ask for the right way."

They all knew he meant that it was not human aid he sought, but that of the Heavenly Father. So he offered a brief prayer and they went forward again, this time successfully, and soon they emerged from the friendly gloom of the forest into the road.

M. Durand extinguished his lantern and gave it to André to carry, shifting Leonie to his other arm, for she was plump and somewhat weighty. Slowly they crept onward, nerves strained, hearts throbbing, their footsteps seemed enough to attract attention, every rustle of leaves, every crackle of a twig made them apprehensive. Once the bushes by the side of the road parted and out sprang a fox. Marie clapped her hands over her mouth to check a scream, for her first thought was that a man was springing on them.

A few moments later footsteps were heard distinctly and Gaston led his party hastily through a gap in the hedge. They all crouched low and waited. The footsteps drew nearer and to their horror a man came close, his dog, that was following him, sprang through the hedge with a low growl. That was more than Ninon could stand and she gave a little cry. All was up. The man followed his dog exclaiming: " What's this ? Who's here ? "

Gaston Durand stood up facing the discoverer, his lips moving in whispered prayer.

The man gave a short laugh.

" Escaping Huguenots, I'll be bound. Well don't worry about me I've got children of my own and I wouldn't harm these little dears. Although I go to mass and confession pretty regularly, I've no use for a religion that persecutes the best in our land. You go your way and I go mine, and nothing need be said by either of us."

" God bless you my friend " Gaston Durand said, and the man saying: " Good luck to you," passed on.

Once again the Durands proceeded and soon the narrow, cobble stone street of the town began. Gaston knew the way well and led them by back alleys to the jetty. They were later than they had meant to be. The church bell was calling the faithful to early prayer, so they knew it was two o'clock. Gaston Durand recalled how it was exactly that hour of the night, more than a hundred years previously, that the ringing of the bell of the church of St. L'Auxerrois had been the signal for the massacre of St. Bartholomew to commence, when the streets of Paris had run with the blood of the martyred Huguenots.

Just for a moment Gaston thought the boat was not there, then to his relief he saw it in the shadow of the wall and presently Captain Hopkin's voice was heard.

" That you Durand ? I began to think you were not coming. Here pass me the little ones."

Leonie was sound asleep and Ninon only half awake. Hopkins placed them on a sail in the bottom of the boat and then handed in Rachelle, Marie and André.

Gaston only waited to see them push off, then he hurried back to the wagon, where at dawn he harnessed the horses and came down openly to the harbour, and soon he and his merchandise was on board.

With what joy Rachelle welcomed her husband, she had been fearful lest something should happen to prevent him joining them, but here he was, and they were all safe on the ship and the sails were set for England.

Chapter VII

ON BOARD "THE VENTURE"

GASTON and Rachelle Durand sat together on deck with hearts too full of thankfulness for words, to express all that they felt at their wonderful escape. At the moment gratitude to God was the uppermost thought in their minds although they knew that possibly many difficulties lay in front of them. To make a fresh start in a strange land, to start business and obtain a livelihood, was a heavy responsibility, but both felt that the God Who had led and protected them so far, would not fail them now.

Rachelle presently said: "Gaston it was wonderful that André should have had that opportunity of helping that soldier, if it had not been for that, the dragoons would have been billeted on us without warning and escape would have been impossible."

"Yes indeed. It was God's provision for us without doubt."

Captain Hopkins here joined them and Rachelle asked innocently: "Are all the English Protestants?"

Captain Hopkins laughed.

"No indeed, Madame. Our King James II who came to the throne early this year is a Catholic and favours his co-religionists. Brought up by his Papist mother, Henrietta of France, he is very bigoted. I fear it will lead to rebellion, for the majority of the people are determined to have a Protestant England. 'Tis but a hundred years ago that the fires of martyrdom glowed on England's soil under Queen Mary, and people haven't forgotten it. Why one of my own ancestors suffered at

Lewes in Sussex, Richard Woodman by name. His daughter Arbel was my great-grandmother."

"Ah that is interesting" Gaston replied.

Marie, André and the little girls gathered round and all were eager to hear all Captain Hopkins could tell them of the land to which they were going.

The captain spoke French with a decidedly English accent and André had to hide a smile occasionally. He was too grateful to the good man to let his amusement be seen, he did not wish to hurt the captain's feelings only sometimes what he said was so funny that André could have laughed aloud.

"Tell us something more about the king?" Rachelle asked.

"Well poor man I think he is to be pitied. He is the second son of the unfortunate King Charles I and was bandied about from place to place during the civil war in his father's reign, consequently he received no regular education. He and his sister Elizabeth were prisoners in St. James' Palace later, placed there by the Parliament. As they were but children they were allowed to play with the Governor's sons and daughters, their favourite game was hide and seek. A Colonel Bamfield was in touch with James and told him to hide very carefully on two or three successive evenings so that his companions might get in the habit of giving up hope of finding him and grow accustomed to missing him for a time. Then one evening when all was planned, James was told to secretly run into the garden as if he were going to hide there, but Bamfield was waiting in the shrubbery and disguising James in a woman's dress, got him away safely to a vessel sailing to Holland and from there after a time to his mother in Paris, where he lived in great poverty."

"Poor lad. And you say his mother was a Papist?" M. Durand asked.

"Yes, that is so. But when James came to the English throne he promised to maintain the laws of the country both in church and state, yet I have heard it rumoured and I fear it is true, that he has dispatched a Catholic priest to Rome to negotiate a reunion with the Papal See. The Pope Innocent XI had more prudence than our king and I am told he has advised our king to do nothing rashly. We have no mind to be paying big sums out of our taxes to support the Pope and his followers, as was done in former days in England. James will need to be careful if he is to keep the throne. But there you ladies look tired and I propose you all get to rest soon. The sea is calm and I hope no one will be ill. Ah what is this, my good man to say a meal is ready. 'Tis but poor fare I fear, but wait till I land you at Rye and take you to my missis, she'll give you some good English food. The thought of it whets my appetite, a big venison pasty, a boar's head in paste, some home-brewed beer and to finish, a good dish of frumenty."

The thought of venison and boar's head did not appeal to Captain Hopkins' passengers but they politely refrained from expressing an opinion on the proposed diet.

Rachelle said: "It is good of you captain to suggest taking us to your home for a meal."

"Madame, you must stay there until you can look round and make your plans."

The conversation continued while they sat round the table, Captain Hopkins asking presently what M. Durand thought of doing when he got to England.

"I propose settling in Canterbury if possible, for some of our religion are already there. They took refuge in your country, sir, a hundred years ago at the time of the massacre of St. Bartholomew."

"Yes, I have heard that is so. And the Huguenots hold their services in the crypt of the cathedral. You will certainly get a welcome there, although there is a service held in the Parish Church at Rye every Sunday for Huguenots and in numerous other places in England. Queen Elizabeth was wise and knew what would benefit her nation. Up to the time of your folks coming to us, wool and the growers were on one side of the Channel and the skilled workmen who dyed and wove it into cloth were on the other. We provided the wool for all the world, but except in a small domestic way of the coarser sorts, most articles of clothing have come to us from France and Flanders. Now the money that we paid to foreign countries for goods is kept circulating in our own land, for your persecuting kings have sent the skilled workmen to us, we could do with many more too."

"Well they are coming in their hundreds now," Gaston replied. "Not only dyers and weavers but men of other trades also."

"'The more the merrier,' is what I say," Captain Hopkins replied, with a hearty laugh. "Look what they have done for our nation, they are thrifty, God fearing, arriving with the desire to earn an honest living. They have good knowledge of trades and occupations unpractised by us. Why it was only the monks who ever did any kitchen gardening, now we are following the example of the imigrants and growing vegetables."

Rachelle's face brightened.

"I'm glad to hear that. I feared I should have to do without my pot herbs for cooking."

"I expect Madame, you will be able to have a garden of your own."

"That's good news, isn't it André ?" Rachelle said turning to her son.

"Why my boy how white you look. What is the matter ?" she continued.

"Ah ! the sea is having an effect on him. You had better take him on deck, Madame," Captain Hopkins advised.

André and his mother disappeared, soon to be followed by Aunt Marie.

Captain Hopkins and M. Durand sat talking a little longer, and referring to their former topic, Captain Hopkins said: "I have heard that good Bishop Latimer once said, 'I wish we could collect together such valuable persons in this kingdom as would be the means of insuring its prosperity.' His wish is being fulfilled. Among the arrival are physicians, mechanics, labourers, hatmakers, potters; near Sandwich they have erected those remarkable mills driven by wind, you know them well I expect, Sir."

"Oh yes, windmills are new in your country, I gather."

"Then there are clockmakers, with pendulums that swing, and printers of paper hangings, which we had never seen before, and the cutlers and jewellers are remarkable for their skill. The secret of felt hat making, they keep a mystery. Only good has come from sheltering them. I read recently a treatise by one Elnathan Parr he wrote, 'England fares the better for showing kindness to the French strangers. Long may England be a sanctuary, a refuge, a harbour for the persecuted saints.' And I also saw a letter sent to the citizens of Norwich by Queen Elizabeth. I made a copy of it for my eldest son, he is a rare scholar and loveth all such documents. I have the copy here and you shall see it."

Captain Hopkins turned to a small chest, and after rummaging for a few moments, he produced a little packet of papers.

"Here 'tis," he said, and then his face fell. "Seems I've lost all but the last page. Blown away when I had it on deck I expect, but this page gives you an idea of the Queen's sentiments."

Gaston Durand took it and read: "Praeing you to continue your favour unto them as long as they shall lyve emongste you qyetlye and obediently to God's treue religion and to her Majesty's lawes, for so one Chrystian man (in charitie) is bound to help another, especially they who do suffre afflixion for the gospelle's sake."

"Interesting indeed," M. Durand replied, and then feeling extremely weary, he asked permission to retire.

"Certainly, certainly, Sir. You have had a week of great anxiety, sleepless nights and not much rest by day. You must get rest now while you can," Captain Hopkins answered.

Chapter VIII

THE ARRIVAL

FORTUNATELY for the travellers the sea kept calm and the sun shone, so their time on board "The Venture," after a few hours of sea sickness, proved pleasant. There was not much wind, so they did not make such speed as the captain could have wished, but he enjoyed long talks with M. Durand, and he was not a man to fret or worry about such a small matter, as taking a few days longer than he had anticipated in reaching Rye.

The last morning the captain sat talking to Rachelle, Gaston and Marie Durand. André was chatting with a sailor and learning all he could about nautical terms and sailing boats. Ninon and Leonie were playing together, for the moment they were agreeing happily, but not out of sight of Madame Durand's watchful eye.

Gaston Durand was looking thoughtful. He had been wondering during this time of intercourse with the jovial, kindhearted captain whether, he, the descendant of a Christian man who had suffered for his faith, the child of a godly mother, was himself a child of God. Gaston felt that God meant him to definitely speak a word in season to the captain about the welfare of his soul.

Captain Hopkins paved the way by saying: "It seems to me a remarkable thing that so many of you Huguenots are willing to lose so much, to pull yourselves up by the roots, so to speak, for the sake of religion. I could never do that I am sure. Live and let live is my motto, do all the good you can to everyone and hope for the best in the next world."

"Friend, it is not for the sake of a religion we act thus, but for the love of our Saviour, Whom we cannot deny.

It is only His grace in our hearts that enables us to do this. May I ask you a question Captain? Do you really feel that when you come to the time when you must meet God, that it will be sufficient to tell Him that you have done all the good you could in this life. Will that be your passport into Heaven?"

Captain Hopkins fidgeted. He gave a little laugh and said: "I'll be bound you and my old mother would agree. She said to me one day, 'Jack, if your good deeds would take you to Heaven, there was no need for Christ to die.' Oh well I daresay 'twill all come right in the end. All these good folk I've helped across the Channel have said, 'We'll pray for you, Captain,' so I expect their prayers will be answered."

Gaston Durand saw that Captain Hopkins was trying to hide his deepest feelings, but there was a wistful look in the man's eye in spite of his light tone of voice, so Gaston said earnestly: "Dear sir, life is so uncertain, do not delude yourself thinking all will come right in the end. Now is the day of salvation, now Christ waits to save you. Delays are dangerous. While we thank God for your good deeds, they will not take you to Heaven; only the Saviour's atoning work on Calvary, accepted by you, can do that. Only His Blood can wash away your sins."

Captain Hopkins was silent awhile then he said: "I don't know that I have ever committed any great sins. I've always tried to live a straight life and, as I said just now, do all the good I can."

"Captain, we need to lay aside our thoughts about sin, and try to enter into what God thinks about it. Calvary is the answer to that, God's beloved Son a sacrifice there because of the hatefulness of sin. God is just and had to deal with sin, in order that man might be pardoned, Christ bore the penalty sin deserved."

Rachelle spoke, she had been listening to her husband's

conversation with the captain.

"It always seems to me a striking thing that when Christ was speaking of the Holy Spirit convincing men of sin, He did not mention what we think of as great sins, but said, 'He will convince the world of sin . . . . because they believe not on Me.' I remember our pastor saying that the word 'believe' there meant a full complete personal trust in the Saviour. So to fall short of that trust, is sin and sin can only be put away by the precious Blood of Christ."

Captain Hopkins arose.

"I must attend to my duties now, but I thank you Madame for your words. If, as you say, that to fail of a full personal trust in the Saviour is sin, then I am indeed a sinner. I must think over what you have said."

"Not far from the Kingdom," Gaston said to his wife.

"Yes indeed. May he not linger there but enter in," Rachelle responded.

Presently Gaston said, "I wonder how the Goyers are faring. Jacques, his wife and daughter were to start off about the time we did. He was at work the last day at home, and he told me he was getting off that evening. I hope they will get safely to Holland and thence to England and finally join us at Canterbury. He is a good workman, I shall be glad when he arrives."

"It is a risky journey for them going by foot, but many others have accomplished it and we must hope that they will get through safely," Rachelle remarked.

A few hours passed and then Captain Hopkins called them to come and see the coast line of England, which was in sight. Soon "The Venture" sailed triumphantly into the little seaport of Rye.

"Let us thank God for all His mercies," Gaston Durand said as they stood on land once more and lifting his cap he offered a few words of thanksgiving for the past and prayer for the future.

CHAPTER IX

COLETTE'S CALL

HOW little the Durands guessed what had really happened to the Goyer family.

Jacques Goyer had gone off to his work that morning with high hopes. His last words to his wife and daughter being: "Only one day more, this evening our start can be made. Everything is ready, Colette ?"

"Everything will be ready by the time you get home, Jacques. I shall be glad now when the wrench of leaving is over."

Colette turned back into the house and she and Jacqueline busied themselves with the final preparations. They were very quiet, scarcely a word was spoken, their hearts were too full for ordinary conversation. Presently Jacqueline standing a moment by the window exclaimed: "Here comes Father Gastigny. What can he want ?"

"My child do not call him 'Father.' God's Word tells us to call no man father on earth, that is in the spiritual sense. Say M. Gastigny dear."

"Yes mother. I forget as everyone calls him that What can he want ?"

"I hope no harm, Jacqueline. You know although M. Gastigny is ignorant of the Gospel as we know it, he is not a bad cruel man. I believe he has done his best to prevent the soldiers doing their wicked work in this neighbourhood, instead of encouraging them as some priests do."

A knock at the door prevented further talk, and Colette Goyer hastened to answer it.

"My daughter, I would have a word with you," the priest said.

"Come in sir," Colette replied.

A frown passed over the man's face, as he noted she refrained from calling him "father."

Colette passed him a chair, but he did not sit down.

"I can only stay a minute," he said, "I have come to warn and advise you. The soldiers are marching hither, in a short time they will be here. Now, take my advice, I have no desire that you and others in this neighbourhood shall suffer death or worse. You will be asked if you will attend mass on the morrow and signify your willingness to abjure your religion. Do not be obstinate. I will not be hard on you nor appoint severe penances if you come into my fold. Colette, do not expose your daughter to insult and injury, for her sake, conform. I am sure Jacqueline, who has ever been an obedient daughter to you, will follow your example."

The old man spoke earnestly and persuasively, and as he looked at Jacqueline in her youthful beauty, his eyes dimmed with tears.

It was a touching scene and Colette Goyer could scarce answer for emotion. For a moment or two she hesitated. Kindness seemed likely to do what persecution could not. But at that moment a Voice sounded in her ear: "They loved not their lives unto the death."

Words she had heard only lately at a Huguenot meeting, held in fear and trembling, and yet ventured on, in order that those who attended might be strengthened to suffer if need be.

"Sir," Colette said, "I cannot promise you this. I only pray that God may give me grace to stand firm, true to Him Who gave His life for me."

M. Gastigny sighed.

"I would fain save you both. I can do no more. I go now to warn others. I advise you to make your escape without delay. I am powerless to help you once the dragonnade has begun. May, Mary, mother of . . ."

Colette interrupted. " Sir, we seek the blessing of God, not that of a woman, who, although blessed indeed of God, was a sinner like ourselves."

The priest hurried away murmuring: " Hopeless, hopeless to try and help them, poor, deluded souls."

" Mother, mother let us fly. Why stay here till the soldiers come. If we can get out to M. Fontaine's farm he will shelter us, and father was going there this evening to fetch the donkey, he will find us there."

" Yes Jacqueline, we will go at once. Just let us kneel in prayer a moment and ask, as we have so often done, that grace and strength may be given us, if we are put to the test."

" Oh mother, I feel so weak; I am afraid I shall fail," Jacqueline moaned.

" Out of weakness made strong. Lean on Christ," Colette said, as she spoke she was putting on her cloak and hood. Jacqueline followed her example. Then they knelt in prayer. It was striking that Colette did not ask so much for safety in their flight as she did for grace to suffer. It seemed almost as though she knew deliverance was not for her. In the days to come, Jacqueline often thought of this.

Suddenly just as they arose from their knees, the noise of tramping feet was heard. Screams of terror from a neighbour's cottage struck on their ears with a note of doom, and Colette and Jacqueline knew escape was impossible.

" Not accepting deliverance," Colette murmured to herself. " Lord help us."

A moment afterwards two burly, coarse looking men opened the door of the cottage.

" Ah, what have we here ? " one said to the other, noting the packages on the table. All ready for flight, my pigeons. May be we'll clip your wings. Now my good woman, are you ready to promise to go to mass to-morrow morn and abjure your religion for the religion of the king ? "

" No, I am not," was Colette's brief reply.

" Come, come now, many of your neighbours are doing this. A little suffering, a burnt arm or a few blows and they are giving in. This pretty girl of yours, if you do not conform we shall take her off to the convent where the sisters will soon convert her. They know how to do it, a taste of their discipine will soon do the trick."

" Don't waste your time, Henri," said the second man. " Now mother, will you or will you not conform ? "

Colette lifted her face bravely. A light shone in her eyes as she said steadily: " I cannot deny my Lord."

For answer the man lifted his heavy musket and with one blow felled her to the ground, where she lay unconscious. The soldier then fired and Colette's spirit took its flight to the Lord, Whose Name she had honoured.

Jacqueline's screams filled the room. The soldiers then turned their attention to her. The man who had killed her mother said: " We shall quickly make a convert of this lass. She'll soon give in and 'tis to our credit to make converts. Here pass your pipe. I'll blow smoke into her eyes, while you hold her hands."

This he proceeded to do. Poor Jacqueline gasped, choked and struggled, but she refused to say the words which would have brought her release. One of the men, growing impatient, gave her a heavy blow on the side of her head nearly stunning her. Whatever cruelty would have followed was checked by the entrance of a young officer. The men turned to him for orders. To their surprise he thundered: " What are you brutes doing ? Hands off."

" She refuses to conform," the soldier said sullenly.

" Then she had better be taken to the Convent and

put in the care of the nuns. Here," turning to a man who had followed him into the cottage—" take this maiden to the others whom you are taking hither."

Jacqueline was led off, trembling and dazed. The blow on her head had almost numbed her senses and she scarcely knew what was happening. She tottered as she walked and presently the man picked her up and carried her to a wagon where a few women and girls were huddled.

These had all refused to give their promise to go to mass on the morrow, and were being taken to the convent.

Meanwhile the young officer stood alone in the Goyer's kitchen.

" It's a miserable business," he said to himself. " I loathe it. That girl ! how she reminded me of my sister. I would fain send in my resignation, but I should be suspected at once of holding Huguenot's views. I suppose a man must put safety first. Ah well, sometimes I am able to save them from the worst, but I've no heart for such work as this."

Chapter X

BAD NEWS FOR JACQUES

THAT same evening Jacques Goyer wended his way home from his daily occupation, eager to join his wife and daughter and make a start on their perilous journey to Holland. He was nearing his house when passing along a narrow street, a voice called his name softly. He stopped, and there in the shadow of a doorway, stood an old decrepit man whom Goyer knew well.

" Goyer, Goyer," he called, " come here a minute."

" What is it ? I'm in a hurry to get home."

" Home, man ! the soldiers have been there. Your wife is killed, may be your daughter too. I don't know."

Jacques staggered. He put his hand on the wall to steady himself. " Is this truth ? " he asked abruptly.

" It is neighbour. I was away most of the day and so escaped as you have. I got back about an hour ago and came out to meet and warn you, for you've done me many a kindness. I thought perhaps you'd better not go on but make your escape while you may."

" I must go on, I must find out if my daughter is alive. I must bury my wife."

Jacques leant against the wall and groaned.

" Oh Colette, wife of my youth, companion of my life, Colette ! "

The slow, painful tears of the middle-aged filled his eyes, only to be brushed aside hastily, as he sought to pull himself together.

" 'Twas a pity she did not conform," the old man said. Jacques turned on him with indignation.

" Man you don't know what you are saying. I am

proud to be the husband of a woman who died for the faith, for the love of our Lord. But I must not linger here. I return to seek my daughter. Did others suffer ? "

" Ah yes. A few were killed, some of the men were taken for the galleys and a number of women, I hear, have been carried off to the Convent."

" Worse than death, worse than death. The galleys and the convent," Jacques murmured as he hastened on. He soon reached his cottage and paused on the threshold, dreading to enter, but after a moment's hesitation he stepped in, half hoping that he would find the old man's story false or at least exaggerated. But no; cold and still, his wife lay, but with a look of serenity on her face that amazed Jacques. He sank on his knees beside his loved one and thanked God that she was safe, at rest, no persecutor could molest her now, no terror reach her.

" Safe home, safe home," he whispered. Then added: " God give me grace to follow in her steps, if need be."

He would fain have lingered there, but he must act. Only at midnight were the Huguenots allowed to bury their dead and Jacques went to seek the aid of a neighbour in preparing a grave for his dear one. The streets were strangely quiet, doors mostly closed, behind which sheltered sad hearts. Either dear ones were missing, or the family had denied their Lord and in either case, sorrow followed. The greater was the sorrow of those who had submitted to their persecutors, for although they were safe from physical torture, yet their hearts were torn, for many of them truly loved the Saviour, although in the moment of temptation they had failed.

Who shall blame them ? When mothers saw their little ones beaten or threatened with convent life, when men witnessed their wives and daughters subjected to indignities worse to bear than death, was it to be wondered at, that in some cases, the word was spoken which sent the soldiers away from the home to leave the family without further punishment.

Jacques knocked at a door. It was cautiously opened and a man peeped out, he whispered: " Come in, Goyer."

" You are all here ? " Jacques said in surprise.

The man hung his head.

" Yes, we have given in; 'Twas the only thing to do."

The wife sitting in a corner broke into sobs. She hugged her child and rocked herself to and fro in misery.

" Poor soul," Jacques said. " Do not forget that although Peter denied His Lord yet he repented and was restored . . . . ."

" Don't man," the father said and Jacques refrained from farther counsel.

" Neighbour, can you help me dig a grave for my wife ? " he asked.

" Yes, yes of course I can," was the reply.

" Have you heard news of your daughter ? " the man continued.

" No, tell me if you know ought. I am going to seek her as soon as . . . ." Jacques broke off with a sob. Then he continued: " Tell me about Jacqueline."

" She and a half-dozen others have been taken to the convent."

Jacques moaned. He had no words for such dire tidings. But he must not stay there. As soon as Colette was buried, he would hasten to the convent, and see if it were possible to do anything for his child.

The night passed only too swiftly and dawn was breaking when Jacques having, with his neighbour's aid, committed the body to the grave, found his way to the convent some three miles outside the town. He was nearing the spot, when suddenly at a turn of the road he found himself confronted by a body of soldiers. Escape was impossible. The usual questions were put to him, liberty was offered him if he would with a few words agree to abjure his faith. Jacques, calmly and quietly refused, and the officer in charge said shortly: "Chain him to one of the other men. The galleys for him."

Goyer was led to a little group of men whom he recognised as his neighbours, one of whom was Pierre Benoit. All were heavily chained and marched forward until they reached an inn where the soldiers stopped for breakfast. The prisoners were left outside and Jacques took the opportunity of speaking to Pierre.

"Pierre, my lad, I grieve to see you here, and yet I rejoice that you have not denied our Lord."

Pierre's face was very white. His voice was husky with emotion, as he whispered: "Jacqueline ! Tell me do you know anything of her ?"

"Alas Pierre, I was hastening to the convent to see if I could find her, for my neighbours told me that she and some other maidens were taken thither."

Pierre groaned, and then in a paroxysm of mental agony he pulled at his chains, he stamped and shouted: "Let me go, let me go. I must find her."

"Hush, hush," several men exclaimed. "Steady my lad, don't rouse the soldiers to anger."

Fortunately the soldiers were too engrossed assuaging their hunger and thirst to notice any noise outside and Pierre ashamed of his sudden outburst, subsided, only sinking to the ground and burying his face in his hands sobbed piteously. An elderly man beside him said: "Courage, courage my boy. The Lord will not forsake you. You will yet rejoice that you were enabled to suffer for His sake. The sufferings of this little while are not worthy to be compared to the glory which is to follow, only let us make sure that we suffer for *love* for Him Who died for us."

He paused, then said suddenly: "My lad, the end is not yet. I have a strong sense within me that deliverance will come to you and your loved one. You can say with the Psalmist 'Why art thou cast down oh my soul? Hope thou in God, for I shall yet praise Him.'"

Nothing more could be said for the innkeeper came out with some food for the prisoners and as soon as that was finished the long weary march began again. On and on to the coast, to take their places among the galley slaves on the Mediterranean.

Chapter XI

THE DESOLATE HOME

IT was a still, summer evening when M. Furneaux with two men servants, rode down the winding avenue that led to his château. A silvery, crescent moon gleamed faintly in the sky. Birds were carolling their evening song; the countryside was quiet; all seemed at peace.

M. Furneaux was in high spirits. Such was his love for his wife and child, he was never willingly absent from them, and now he was anticipating a happy reunion. He turned to his faithful servant, Jean, who rode beside him saying: "Home in a few minutes Jean, and then in a day or two we'll be off to Geneva. I know no peace here, we've seen enough on our journey to make us feel that it is only at a distance from Paris and out of reach of that vile persecutor, King Louis, can we know any safety."

"Eh, eh, Master. That is so. I tell you Sir, when I saw that group of lasses being hastened to the convent and those young men doomed to the galleys, as we did a few days ago, I was thankful that I have neither wife nor child."

M. Furneaux laughed heartily. "Ah, you old bachelor, I don't envy you. And if you have neither wife nor child, I know Madame Furneaux and little Leonie are as much objects of your devotion and care as if they were your own."

"Eh, eh, Master, that's true, and glad I'll be to have them safe over the border."

"Here Martin, where's your hautboy, give a tune and rouse the folks and let them know we're coming."

Martin, the second man, nothing loath to obey his master, blew a mighty blast, and within a few minutes the three men rode into the courtyard of the château.

The strange silence caused a feeling of chill and foreboding to M. Furneaux's heart. Where were the stable men, and footmen and various servants that always flocked to greet the master on his arrival?

M. Furneaux shouted as he descended from his horse flinging the rein to Jean. Still there was no response. Then after a moment a door cautiously opened and an old woman servant peeped out. She threw the door widely open when she saw who had arrived and with a cry, partly of pain, partly of pleasure, buried her face in her hands and sobbed.

M. Furneaux strode towards her exclaiming: "What is it Nanette? What has happened? Where is your lady? Tell me, tell me, woman."

The icy grip of fear that he had first experienced took firmer hold. Something terrible had happened, he felt sure. He rushed into the hall and was about to mount the staircase saying as he went: "Is your lady ill Nanette? Speak, speak quickly."

The old woman with a tremendous effort pulled herself together.

"Master, master, it was the dragonnade. The soldiers came and our mistress was shot."

M. Furneaux reeled and might have fallen, had not Jean who had followed him into the hall, caught him in his arms and placed him on a chair.

He groaned in anguish.

"My wife, my beautiful darling gone."

Then he lifted his head. "But Leonie, my child, what of her?"

"Alas master, Marthé sought to escape with her, but Marthé was caught and later shot and thrown into the moat, and they tell me the little mistress was found dead on the road."

"And the rest of you?"

The old woman mentioned several names of her fellow servants, explaining that some had been killed, one or two of the men taken for the galleys, some of the women to the convent.

"And you? How is it you escaped?" M. Furneaux asked.

"Alas master! I was weak and when they threatened me I said the words they wished me to. Alas! I have fallen low."

"'Tis the only thing to do, Nanette. The Lord hath dealt hardly with me. I have lost my faith. I shall go to the priest and conform, then I shall at least be left in peace. Jean and Martin you had better do the same."

M. Furneaux sat lost in sad thought until Jean brought food and tried to rouse him. Scarcely knowing what he did, he ate and drank mechanically. Later he inquired of Nanette what had happened to the bodies of his loved ones and his servants. Nanette told him that a neighbour M. de Monceau, whose château was about three miles off, had come and superintended the burial.

"I have heard since, master, that M. de Monceau has also suffered, but I know not if it is true. He was of the faith."

"Yes, a good man. Happy for him if he, his wife and son all went together. To be left to face life without wife or child is the deepest sorrow. The brutes, the villains to murder even a little innocent child!"

Old Nanette could give no word of comfort she had no idea that the child found killed on the road was not Leonie. She was a motherless child whose father had been taken from his work to the galleys. Left alone in her cottage home, child-like she had run out into the road on hearing the tramp of men and horses and had run straight into the baggage wagon. One of the heavy wheels had passed over her head and body, destroying her features and mangling her clothes.

The soldiers had flung the little, lifeless body on to the side of the road and when later it was discovered, M. de Monceau took it for granted that the child was little Leonie Furneaux.

After spending a few restless days M. Furneaux rode off to visit the home of the M. de Monceau. He found the report that Nanette had given him was true. M. and Madame de Monceau had suffered for the Faith. M. Furneaux did not linger there, he turned away, sad at heart, to go back to his home now only a dwelling place. He had not gone many yards towards the spot where his horse was tethered, when he heard a voice calling him.

" M. Furneaux, Sir, stop a moment, I beg of you."

He turned and saw a peasant woman following him. He knew her to be the wife of a charcoal burner in the woods, on M. de Monceau's estate.

" What is it dame ? " he inquired.

She looked nervously around and beckoned to him to follow her, which he did. The woman plunged into the wood, now and again turning round to see if M. Furneaux was coming after her along the narrow, winding track. Presently she paused and waiting for M. Furneaux to come close to her she said: " No one will hear us here. I saw you going into the master's château and I said, 'The Lord be praised, M. Furneaux will help me.' "

" What is it you want ? " M. Furneaux again asked.

The woman still looked anxiously around, apparently fearful to speak, even in this secluded spot. Then lowering her voice she said: " I've saved the little master. He is here in our hut."

" The little master ! You mean Henri de Monceau ? "

" Yes, yes sir. I was up at the château when I saw

the soldiers coming . Master Henri was in the kitchen garden, I knew. I rushed there to save him, for he was my foster child, I brought him up with my own son and I loved him. So I hastened him away through the woods and have kept him hidden these ten days, but my humble cot is no place to bring up a little seigneur."

"No, indeed, but you were a wise woman to act as you did. Now I will take Henri to my home, he shall be my son for I have lost my wife and daughter."

"Alas, alas, sir ! I had heard a rumour of that. 'Tis terrible times we live in. I will fetch the little master, he will be glad to see you. He is fretting badly about his father and mother. I had to tell him for he would have rushed back to the château."

M. Furneaux followed the woman into the hut and found Henri de Monceau sitting on a heap of straw looking disconsolate.

He sprang up when he saw who the visitor was and exclaimed joyfully "Oh Monsieur, I am glad to see you. Is it true that I shall never see my parents again ?"

"I will be your father, Henri. I have come to take you home with me."

"To be with Madame and little Leonie. Oh I am glad."

M. Furneaux's face contracted with a spasm of anguish and he could not reply for a moment or two. Then he said slowly: "We are alike, Henri. You have lost your parents, I have lost my wife and child. We must comfort one another."

Henri impulsively flung his arms around M. Furneaux exclaiming: "We will, we will. I will be good, Monsieur."

"Call me 'Father,' Henri. You are to be my son. Come we will go home now."

M. Furneaux rewarded the woman with a louis d'or

for her kindness and told her to come and see her foster son when she felt so inclined.

So the two went off, and reaching M. Furneaux's horse they mounted, Henri riding in front of his adopted father; child-like, for the moment he forgot his sorrow and chatted merrily.

One of the first things M. Furneaux did was to take Henri to the priest and arrange for him to be received into the Roman Catholic church. Some boys of Henri's age—for he was ten years old, would have protested. Children did so in many parts of France in that time of persecution and suffered for their faith.*

But Henri had not received the grace of God into his heart. Two thoughts filled his mind and controlled his actions. One was the desire to please his adopted father and the other to make himself safe from persecution and suffering.

Henri's disposition would always lead him to take the easy path and make himself agreeable to those with whom he had to associate, as long as his own wishes were not crossed.

* "A record has been found at Toulon of a boy of twelve being sent to the galleys for having accompanied his parents to a preaching." *The Huguenots*, by SAMUEL SMILES.

CHAPTER XII

THE CONVENT

A GROUP of merry light-hearted girls sat in a large rather bare room in the convent at Niort where they were being educated. It was the one hour in the day when they were free to laugh and talk without much supervision. It was true, a young nun, Sister Marie Tryphena, sat with them, but the girls were quite indifferent to her presence. She sat with her eyes fixed on an elaborate piece of embroidery which she was working and found it easier for her own peace of mind, to ignore the conversation going on around her, and to report at the end of the hour, when her charges would go to the refectory for supper, that all had behaved well.

"Where is Stephanie ?" one girl suddenly asked.

"Spying out something, you may be sure" was the answer at which most of the girls laughed.

Stephanie's chief characteristic was an inordinate curiosity, she was always trying to fathom some mystery, find out some secret and then bring a thrill to her schoolmates by announcing her discovery, usually much exaggerated and highly coloured, in order to create a sensation.

Almost as the girls spoke, the door of the room opened and Stephanie entered.

"Girls, girls, such excitement. The soldiers have brought a party of heretic women and girls here, they are in the courtyard now. If you come to the gallery window you can all have a peep at them, such fun."

The girls immediately started off with Stephanie. The poor little nun in charge made a mild protest, but not one of the girls took any heed, and after a moment's hesitation, the nun followed her charges and went also to the gallery window.

The pretty girlish faces were pressed against the panes, eager to see the new comers. Many were the exclamations.

" Oh look at that old woman, she is fainting."

" See that girl, her face is bruised."

But more than one said: " Look Catherine, do look at that girl on the edge of the group, she is like you, goldy-brown hair, dark eyes and there is something about her figure and the shape of her face that is like yours."

" Sure she isn't a long lost sister of yours ? " another girl asked laughingly.

" I never had a sister," Catherine de Vere answered. " What a dear the girl looks, What a shame to persecute her."

" It's not persecuting," one girl protested, " It is for their good, to convert them to the true faith."

The girls were suddenly interrupted in the conversation by a scared whisper from Sister Marie Tryphena. She was dividing her attention between the scene in the courtyard and the hall below. From the gallery she could see the entrance hall, door and staircase, and she caught sight of a black robed figure approaching.

" Girls, girls, someone is coming ! " she said in a low whisper.

Only too well she knew the blame of this adventure would fall on her. She would be taken to task for allowing her charges to leave the schoolroom until the time came for them to get ready for supper.

The authorities were fairly indulgent to these young daughters of the wealthy homes of France. Only a few years previously Sister Marie Tryphena had been one of them, but now she had taken the veil, and incidently brought considerable dowry to the convent, she was no longer of any importance. Fortunately for her the girls were good natured although thoughtless, and moreover were fond of the gentle little Sister, so they followed her back to the schoolroom and were seated demurely occupied with various bits of needlework, when a nun entered saying: "The Abbess requests the presence of Mademoiselle Catherine de Vere at once."

Catherine jumped up with an exclamation of surprise and some of her schoolfellows asked: "What have you been doing, Catherine?"

"Nothing, that I can think of, perhaps it is not to scold me. You see I am going home soon and it might have something to do with my escort."

"Don't be too sure," someone warned.

The nun who had brought the message could have told the reason, but she did not feel inclined to satisfy the girl's curiosity.

Catherine hurried to the Abbess' parlour and was delighted to find her brother had come and was asking permission to see his sister. Catherine was a great favourite with the Abbess and now she shewed her partiality by graciously permitting Catherine to join her brother in the garden, rather than, as was usual, receive him in a small room where a nun would sit and hear all the conversation.

"Your brother, my child, is in the pleasance. He is in this neighbourhood on the king's errand to suppress the terrible Huguenots who abound around this district. A good deed, which will bring him reward both in this life and in the next."

Catherine was eager to join her brother and did not wish to linger to hear the Abbess' views on this subject. She only waited for the words: "You may go now and join M. le Capitaine," and swiftly she hastened into the garden.

Her brother, her only brother René, an officer in the

king's own regiment, whom she loved dearly, what joy it was to see him.

The two embraced warmly. Then Catherine drew back to have a good look at René.

"Oh René, you look tired and white. I do hope you are not ill."

"No little one, I am well, but I am sick of my job, I am not made for this kind of work. If I were sent to fight the Moors and Turks, may be I could face it, but women and children, men too, who are innocent of treason or crime, of our own nationality; I sicken of it. Here let us sit down on this seat, it seems secluded."

"Yes, but do be careful René, it would never do for your remarks to be heard. Could you not send in your resignation and come home? There would be plenty to occupy you on our estate and father would be delighted to have you. Do consider this?"

René smiled. "Nothing I should like better. I am cut out for a quiet country squire, not a soldier, but I should be suspected of having become a Huguenot and Louis would show me no mercy. Did you know I was at Court a few weeks ago?"

"Yes, I had a letter from father in which he told me. How did you like it?"

"I loathed it. It is a vile place. The king is a bigoted persecutor, short sighted in his policy and will bring his country to ruin it seems to me. He is completely under the thumb of the Jesuits and Madame de Maintenon who nurses him."

"Is he ill?"

"Yes indeed, his body is decaying, he has lost his teeth, he has a disease in the jaw bone, and as for his character, well I can't speak of that. He is horrible to his wife and altogether I was thankful when my time at Court expired."

"And now you have to rout out these Huguenots.

You do not think them very wicked ? "

" No certainly not. I do not understand their religion but they seem to be quiet, hardworking people, their homes are happy and they cling to one another, and my job, mine alas ! is to step in and destroy these homes, send the men to the galleys and the women and girls to convents. I am glad to say my hands are clean from bloodshed, but I have not been able to prevent the soldiers from killing some. They know the king's orders to proceed to extreme measures if persuasion fails to make converts. And all this in the name of religion. Louis is spoken of as 'Most Christian King.' And Madame Maintenon wrote a letter saying: 'The King is prepared to do everything that shall be judged useful for the welfare of religion; this undertaking will cover him with glory before God and man.' "

' It does seem too bad. I can't understand religion at all, can you René ?

" I don't want to have anything to do with it, I can tell you. By-the-bye Catherine, one of the Huguenot girls I came across to-day and rescued from two brutal soldiers, reminded me of you."

Catherine exclaimed.

" Why I believe she is here. We were looking out of the window and saw a number of women and girls in the courtyard and several of my schoolmates pointed out a girl as being like me."

" I expect that is the one I mean. I gave orders that the women and girls were to be brought here. The Abbess and nuns fancy themselves good at making conversions."

René spoke wearily.

" Oh René ! They will be terribly hard on the poor things. That pretty girl. I wish I could help her. Oh I know what I can do. When I leave here next month I'll ask the Abbess to let me have her for my maid. I am rather a favourite. I might be able to persuade her."

"You will if you offer to make a good contribution to the convent funds, I daresay."

René de Vere laughed mockingly.

Then the conversation turned to other matters. Catherine was full of eager anticipation of the time now drawing near, when she was to leave the convent school, and go home to her father. Her mother had died when she was quite young and Catherine was tenderly loved by both her father and brother, an affection which she warmly reciprocated.

While this interview was taking place the poor, weary, heartsick women and girls, who had been brought to the convent, were being placed in bare, comfortless cells. The convent was an immense building and cells were numerous, so the Abbess gave orders that each girl and woman was to be alone. She was a great believer in the corrective power of solitude and she determined to be in no hurry to take any other steps to promote "conversion" for the present, than that of leaving each victim severely alone. Once a day a silent nun brought a ration of sour, rye-bread and a pitcher of water. Far from the sound of human voice in an almost dark cell, for only a tiny grating admitted air or light, so that for most of the twenty-four hours it was dark, with only the bare, cold floor on which to rest, the Abbess felt resistance against her will would soon wear away.

Poor Jacqueline, who was one of the girls, lay on the floor too dazed for thought, for she was still suffering from the blow she had received on the head, but as the hours passed, she roused herself from her semi-conscious condition and the terribleness of her position overwhelmed her with a poignant grief. Tears came and she hid her face in her hands sobbing bitterly. Jacqueline had always had a horror of the dark and the black gloom seemed to press on her eyeballs, giving her the feeling that she had lost her sight. Whether it was day or night she could not tell, but she felt she could have screamed aloud for a light. Poor girl if she had, no one would have heard her, and her piteous sobs reached no human ear. But the Heavenly Father hears the cry of the helpless and some words Jacqueline had heard read at a Huguenot gathering came to her mind with a great sense of comfort.

" The city had no need of the sun for the Lamb was the Light thereof." Jesus said: " I am the Light of the world." Jacqueline remembered too how the pastor had read other words, the prayer of the Psalmist: " Lord lift up the Light of Thy Countenance upon us."

The words fell on her troubled spirit with healing calm.

" The Lamb is the Light thereof," she whispered to herself.

Then she prayed, asking for grace to suffer, if it should be God's will for her. She thought of her father and Pierre and consoled herself with the thought that they both would do their best to rescue her.

Poor Jacqueline. Perhaps it was well that she did not know that both her father and Pierre were marching away, away from the neighbourhood in chains, each step taking them farther from the girl they would have helped had it been in their power. There was no aid to come from them, but Jacqueline's Heavenly Father was planning for her in a way she knew not.

CHAPTER XIII

CANTERBURY

THE Durands were glad indeed when they at last reached Canterbury, Mistress Hopkins had welcomed them warmly and done her best to make them feel at home for the few days they spent with her and the captain in their home at Rye. But Gaston Durand was anxious to get on as soon as possible, and when the rather tedious preparations were made for the journey, they made a start. A wagon was hired drawn by six horses placed one before another. The service of a guide was secured and two men to go along with them as "way-menders." All this was expensive work, but there was no other way suitable for M. Durand and his family to travel. True stage-coaching had begun a few years previously, in spite of strenuous resistance from those who held that it would make men effeminate and deprive thousands of a means of livelihood, but the public stage-coach would not have conveyed M. Durand's loom and household goods, to say nothing of the well filled bags containing louis d'or.*

After some days of travel, delayed at times by the wagon getting into ruts and pits, also by the guide, who, having made great assertions that he knew every step of the way, led them wrongly, they finally sighted the towers of the Cathedral at Canterbury. It was towards evening and they were glad to make their way to the

* "The French Ambassador in England wrote to Louis XIV in 1687 that as much as 960,000 louis d'or had been sent to the Mint for conversion into English money. See SMILES' *Huguenots.*

pilgrim's inn called: "The Chequers of the Hope," and get a rest.

Next day Gaston lost no time in seeking a permanent home and was delighted to find an empty house in St. Peter's Street. It was fairly commodious and contained one room large enough to take the loom. The house faced the narrow cobble-stoned street and backed on the river Stour. Having been through the house he hastened back to "The Chequers of the Hope," and brought his wife and family to see what they thought of their future home. Rachelle felt a pang of longing for the spacious rooms of the old home in France, the sunny courtyard, the kitchen garden, but she bravely hid her feelings reminding herself of how little she and her family had suffered for the faith in comparison with others of her co-patriots, so she entered warmly into Gaston's schemes; smiled at the children's delight that some of their back windows looked on the river and they would be able to watch the boats going up and down; compared ideas with her sister-in-law as to how they would furnish and allot the bedrooms, and generally succeeded in setting a happy tone to their new adventure.

Before many days passed they had made their home ready and taken possession. They settled in finally on a Saturday, and Sunday morning saw them all at the beautiful cathedral. There they found a number of their fellow countrymen gathered for worship in the Undercroft, originally known as "The Lady Undercroft Chapel." It had been a gorgeous shrine containing a statue of the Virgin Mary of pure gold, over which hung a canopy starred with jewels and precious stones, with a row of silver lamps hanging from the roof; that was before Henry VIII took possession of the gold, silver, and jewels of the cathedral and converted them into money.

For a time the undercroft was deserted and became merely a large vaulted, ill-lighted area, but now on the Sunday when the Durands first visited it, it was a place of worship. It was roomy, extending under the choir and high altar of the cathedral and the exiles were thankful for the refuge it afforded them and they daily gathered there to sing praises to God for the deliverance given them and to read the Scriptures and pray. The Durands were quick to notice the texts of Scriptures, in their own language, taken from the Psalms, Proverbs and New Testament, inscribed over the capitals of the columns on the north side of the crypt.

It was nearly time for the worship to start, so the Durands sat down on a bench. There was a ceremony that morning that impressed them all. A little group of people, who, before they succeeded in making their escape from France had been forced to attend mass; terrified by threats, seeing the suffering of those who stood firm, they had yielded to their persecutors, only to repent with bitter tears, that they like Peter of old, had denied their Lord. On reaching England their first act was to seek out a Pastor and tell of their sin. In these cases, and there were many, public acknowledgement of the wrong had to be made, before they could be received into the church and allowed to join with others at the Lord's Table. So now this morning a family, broken-heartedly made their confession and were received into the fellowship. Very tender were the pastor's words as he addressed the penitents. Many were there who knew how strong the temptation had been and how nearly they themselves had come to the point, where they, except for the grace of God, would have fallen also.

After the service was over the new comers were warmly welcomed, and they felt more at home than any moment on English soil.

Gaston and Rachelle were glad to find that a week day school for French boys was held in part of the undercroft and André's name was enrolled as a pupil. André was a little disappointed at this, he had thought his lesson-days were over and he would now take his place in his father's workroom, but M. Durand, himself a fairly well educated man, was anxious that his son should have at least another year of schooling. Anything the little girls were to learn must be taught them at home. The majority of middle-class women were entirely uneducated, Marie Durand, could neither read nor write, and in the opinion of her brother was none the worse for that. Rachelle did not altogether share his opinion on the matter, she herself could read, and loved a few rare moments of leisure to read the Bible, so she desired that Ninon and Leonie should both have some education.

She pointed out to her husband that Leonie Furneaux as the daughter of a rich man would have received tuition on various subjects so they ought to give her any advantage they could. Gaston was always ready to listen to his wife and they had not been in their new home long, before Gaston came in contact with an elderly French immigrant, M. Perrier, who was in great poverty. Gaston was delighted to kill two birds with one stone, provide a tutor for his little girls and a livelihood for the old man at the same time. Four-year-old Leonie was too young to learn much more than writing and reading, but Ninon's studies included geography, chronology, and the Copernican system of the vortex and the plainer problems of the globe. M. Perrier was an aristocrat and although his surcoat was threadbare yet it was scrupulously clean, and he still wore a small lace cravat carefully darned, and his wig was large. He was a gentle soul and Ninon and Leonie soon became fond of him.

One morning when they had been having lessons for

a month, Madame Durand was surprised to find Ninon in tears. The tutor had just gone. Madame Durand put her arm around her little daughter and asked what was wrong. Ninon's sobs grew louder and at first her mother could not understand what she was saying. Presently to her amazement she caught the words: " I hate Leonie, I hate Leonie."

Leonie was standing near. Her big eyes filled with wonderment. Whatever her crime had been, she seemed unconscious of it.

Madame Durand felt it wise to say: " Leonie darling, run and find Aunt Marie, she is working with such pretty wools this morning, you will like to help her pick them out."

Leonie ran off to the big workroom, she loved to watch the shuttles flying, colour was a great pleasure to her, for she had a strong artistic sense, also she was already a favourite with the few workpeople whom M. Durand had gathered round him. She was beginning to chatter in English and seemed to the rather stolid men and women, like a flash of sunshine or a brilliant hued butterfly. When Leonie was gone, Ninon sobbed out her story. M. Perrier had taken Leonie on his knee and kissed her and had not shown a similar favour to Ninon.

Madame Durand sighed. Jealousy again !

" Darling," she said, " Leonie is such a little girl, you are growing a big, tall girl, it is only because Leonie is so small that M. Perrier pets her. I am sure he is kind to you also."

" You all love Leonie best. André does. He brought her two lovely blue bird's eggs yesterday and he did not give me one."

Again the mother sighed. She had noticed André's tenderness toward Leonie while to Ninon, hefty and rather plain, he was inclined to be brusque.

"Ninon dear, you must not think André does not love you, he treats you like a big girl, a comrade, and Leonie as a baby. Darling, you will make mother very sad if you give way to jealousy. It is a serious thing to say you hate Leonie, poor child she has no kind father nor mother. I hope you will be very sorry for letting such hard thoughts come into your heart and such wrong words into your lips."

"Oh Mother, do go on loving me," poor Ninon said.

Madame Durand put her arm around the child and held her fast.

"My darling, Mother will always love her little daughter, but she does not love the naughty temper and jealousy and that is like Jesus, He loves you, but he does not love the sin."

"Was it sin?" Ninon asked aghast.

"Yes Ninon," her mother answered firmly. "I hope you will go to your bedroom and kneel down and ask Jesus to forgive you and put His love into your heart for Leonie."

Ninon went off to her bedroom, climbing the black, oak staircase to the attic she shared with Leonie. Presently she came back with a penitent little face and Madame Durand greeted her cheerfully, saying she was going to do some shopping and Ninon could come with her.

Rachelle Durand was getting hold of some English phrases, her husband and M. Perrier being always ready to help her. The shopkeepers knew some French having learnt from the immigrants who were already in Canterbury, so Rachelle did not do too badly.

To-day she went to the butcher with her basket intent on getting an oxtail. It was a little time before she could get the good-natured, stout, rosy-cheeked butcher to understand her request, when he did, he laughed heartily and turning to his assistant exclaimed : "Madame wants an oxtail. What can she be going to do with that ? "

Then he explained that the oxtails went with the hides to the tanneries and were always thrown away, but if she went to the slaughter house she could probably rescue one or two. This she did, and brought home two fine ones in triumph for her pot-au-feu.

Soon the butcher arranged to have the oxtails on sale, and thus the English people learnt from the French immigrants, the value of oxtail for food and soup.

Chapter XIV

JOHN GILES

THE months passed happily for the Durands in their new home, but they did not forget their own land and the friends they had left behind them. When the Summer was over and Winter had followed Autumn, they began to fear for the safety of their good foreman Jacques Goyer. He, his wife and daughter should have reached them ere this, had all gone well. Two of their workmen, with wives and children had succeeded in getting to them and were installed at work. Gaston Durand having bought a large barn for the looms he had had made, the room in the home not being sufficient for his employees and plant.

In spite of the uprooting which they had experienced, the Durands were content and thankful, although quite willing to make new friends they were all-sufficient in themselves as a family, for happiness. Now the Winter evenings had come they made a pleasant picture gathered round the log fire in the room on the ground floor of their home. One evening they were gathered thus, André was roasting chestnuts, Ninon seated by her mother puckering her brows and every now and again putting the tip of her little red tongue out of her mouth, in her efforts to successfully accomplish a piece of embroidery; she was quite good with her fingers and enjoyed using a needle more than studying a book. Gaston Durand had a book in his hands but his reading did not progress very rapidly, as he seemed to prefer watching the various members of his family and listening to what they were saying. Leonie flitted from one to another, now hanging over André as he sat on the rug in front of the fire, now leaning against M. Durand's arm, then picking up the big, black cat and hugging him until he struggled out of her embrace. Rachelle and Marie were knitting thick, warm stockings for the children's wear.

Presently a knock on the outer door was heard and Gaston went to open it. A farmer with whom Gaston had done business stood there, he apologised for calling in the evening after business hours but as he happened to be in Canterbury he had taken the opportunity of letting M. Durand know he could deliver a load of fleeces at any time, when it was convenient for M. Durand to receive them.

Gaston asked him to come in.

" It is too cold to stand in the doorway, Mr. Giles. Come in and get a warm before you start for home."

Mr. Giles followed Gaston into the family room and was introduced to Rachelle and Marie.

He looked so cold that Gaston suggested a hot drink, and Rachelle asked if he would like to try the new China drink.

" Some people call it China tay or toe, I am told. I find it refreshing although my husband does not like it, he prefers a cup of chocolate."

" The fact is I have a sweet tooth, so like the chocolate best," Gaston said.

" The China drink can be sweetened with a little honey if people like it in that way," Rachelle explained.

Mr. Giles replied that it was very kind of the lady to offer the new drink but he would prefer the chocolate.

Marie got up to prepare it, saying softly to her sister-in-law: " I'll get it Rachelle, I know you are tired."

Mr. Giles eyes followed Marie as she moved around. She fetched a skillet from the kitchen, cleared a little spot in the front of the fire and placed the skillet there, with some water in it to boil. She took a delightful old mug from the cupboard and mixed the chocolate and finally brought it to the boil in the skillet.

Placing the mug on a tray with a plate containing a French massepan (a kind of biscuit) she put it on a little table in front of Mr. Giles, who murmured: " Thank ye, m'm."

Had he been a Frenchman he would have risen and bowed politely, but John Giles would have said he had no use for dandified ways.

Presently he took his leave, Gaston Durand accompanying him to the door having arranged for the delivery of the fleeces without delay.

John Giles lingered a moment saying with a wistful note in his voice: " Yon's a pretty scene, Mister. A man's happy to have what you have."

" Eh indeed. I am that. Look in again and share our family party Giles."

" You must bring your folk out to the farm when the Spring comes on," Mr. Giles replied and M. Durand said he would be delighted to do so.

Meanwhile inside, Rachelle and Marie were discussing the visitor. " What a grave looking man, I might say stern," Rachelle said.

" Poor man," Marie added, " did you notice his eyes Rachelle ? They were so wistful. They reminded me of our old dog at home, his eyes had that expression when anyone scolded him. I fancy life is hard for poor Mr. Giles in some way."

Ninon surprised them all by saying: " Like it is for me."

André laughed merrily and Ninon's eyes filled with tears.

" Don't André," Madame Durand said. She put her arm around Ninon and said lightly: " We've all got our trials, Ninon."

' Leonie is my trial," Ninon said and before her mother could speak Leonie exclaimed: " I'm not a trial, I'm a pet, a dear, pretty little girl, lots of people say so."

Madame Durand sighed. Leonie was so pretty, so quick in the uptake and fascinating, that people unwisely said flattering things to her and already Leonie was showing that she loved these remarks. Only that morning Marie had seen her climb on a chair and look in a mirror remarking complacently to herself: " I'm glad I'm a pretty girl."

Madame Durand now spoke gravely. " Leonie you won't be a dear little girl if you are conceited and vain. Nice girls don't think about their looks. Proud thoughts soon spoil the face. Our looks are influenced by what we think."

Leonie did not like her adopted mother to speak in this grave way although she did not entirely understand the remarks. She flung herself on Madame Durand's lap with a pouting mouth and tear-filled eyes.

" You don't love poor, little Leonie."

" I do love Leonie and I want her to be good and kind." Madame Durand said. " It's bedtime now dearie so say 'goodnight.' Aunt Marie is putting you to bed to-night."

The child went off with Marie and even as she ascended the stairs, they heard her merry laugh ring out. Leonie could not be sad or serious for many minutes. Directly she was gone André who had hugged and kissed her before she left said: " Mother, Leonie is right, she is a pet and a pretty child. It is silly of Ninon not to like her. It's just jealousy because she herself is not so pretty."

Madame Durand spoke sharply.

" André, you are old enough to know it is not wise to make remarks like that. You won't help your sister that way."

Ninon was in tears and Madame Durand wondered if she had brought a cuckoo into the family nest. How difficult it was to train children, she felt unequal to the task. Perhaps she was not strict enough, she knew in most families, children were not allowed the freedom of speech that she permitted her children and young people were thrashed severely for the slightest fault or even without a fault, simply because flogging was supposed to be good for them.

Madame Durand took Ninon to bed shortly after and when she was tucked into her little trundle bed her mother sat beside her. Ninon nestled down and gave a sigh of satisfaction. Madame did not often sit beside the child when she had gone to bed and it pleased her.

" Ninon, do you remember your little garden that was all your own at home and how careful you were to keep it free from weeds ? "

Rachelle Durand still spoke of France as " home."

" Yes," Ninon said wonderingly. " I wish I had a garden here."

" You have a garden Ninon. It is the little garden of your heart, and I am afraid you are letting the weeds grow there."

Ninon's eyes were wide open with a look of surprise.

" What kind of weeds ? " she whispered.

" Unkind thoughts, jealousy, hatred. All very ugly weeds that will choke the good things if they are allowed to grow. I hope, Ninon, that you have given the little garden of your heart to Jesus and He wants it to be beautiful with love, kindness, humility, growing there."

The tears came into Ninon's eyes, for she did love Jesus and in spite of her many faults of character wanted to please Him.

" I think of it like this sometimes," Madame Durand continued, " God is looking down on this world and He sees so many ugly things that pain Him, so when He looks into my heart I want it to be a joy to Him, something there that will give Him pleasure. You want that too, don't you darling ? "

" Oh yes, I do," Ninon said.

Her mother's gentle talk was doing far more for her than any scolding or punishment could have done. Before leaving the child Madame Durand read a verse from the Bible." " Instead of the thorn shall come up the fir tree, and instead of the brier shall come up the myrtle tree."

And Ninon understood that Christ could give her plants of joy instead of weeds in her heart. She flung her arms around her mother saying, " I'm so glad you love me mother. I do want to be good like you."

" Ask Jesus to make you like Him, dear."

When Rachelle returned to the living room she asked her husband if he knew anything of Mr. Giles' home-life.

" No nothing whatever," Gaston replied. " I have only had business relations with him in the market place. But he has invited us to come and see him as soon as the weather is better and the roads less muddy."

" I think he looks terribly forlorn, as if he wanted mothering," Marie remarked. Her brother laughed.

" Ah, you always want to be mothering someone or something Marie, if it is only a stray kitten."

Marie stooped and patted the cat.

" Well my stray kitten has repaid my care. He is a beautiful cat and a good mouser."

Madame Durand had yet another talk with a member of her family before bedtime. She pointed out to André what mischief his unwise remarks would do, but she found she need not say much, for the boy was extremely penitent and promised to be careful in the future.

Next morning as he had a holiday he sought to make amends to Ninon by suggesting he should take her for a walk. Ninon's face grew rosy with pleasure and she hurried to her mother for permission which was easily obtained. Madame Durand was pleased and she watched them off with a smile on her face, and mother-like thought how charming they looked. Ninon's animated expression made her look another child than when she was pouting with a look of wounded pride or sullen jealousy. She wore a dress of warm cloth woven in her father's workroom, it reached to her ankles and over it she wore a red cloak and bonnet, the latter having a pleating of lace around the face.

The two went down the street crossing the bridge till they reached the White Friars, then turned at right angles leaving the town by Queengate, passed St. Augustine's Abbey and hence out into the fields.

It was a frosty morning so they were not inconvenienced by mud. André exerted himself to give his sister a pleasant morning and succeeded. Ninon remembered it for long and her little heart which had an intense craving for love and appreciation was warmed and comforted.

CHAPTER XV

JOHN GILES' HOME

IT was not until the Spring was well advanced that Gaston Durand took his wife to visit Mr. Giles. Although the farm was only a couple of miles out of Canterbury, the road was so bad, so thick with mud in the winter, so uncertain with ruts and holes, that no one travelled it for pleasure, only on business.

John Giles had been in once or twice to the Durand's home and seemed to like coming. Now that the Spring winds and sunshine had dried the mud, there seemed no reason why Gaston and Rachelle Durand should not accept the invitation and visit Heathmoor Farm. John Giles had asked them all to come, but Rachelle realising that the invitation had come from the man of the house and not from the old mother whom they understood kept house for him, decided that two were enough for that first visit. John Giles had said little about his home, they only knew that he had lost his wife, and thought that he and his mother were the only inmates of the house. They were surprised to find there were two children, a boy of twelve and a girl of eight.

Mistress Giles, a stately old lady with white hair received them. She was plainly dressed, but the dull brown cloth of which her gown was made was a good material, the kind known as "sayes." Over it she wore an apron of silk taffeta, round her waist she wore a girdle from which hung a bunch of keys, her dress was finished at the neck with a broad linen collar. Her expression was so severe that Rachelle felt shy. She had an idea that Mrs. Giles was looking at her with stern disapproval, and later when she knew the old lady better, she had no doubt that this was so. Rachelle Durand could no more help making her garments dainty and putting them on with a pretty grace, than a poppy can help its gay hue or a rose its beauty. It was not that she gave undue thought or time to her dressing, but a natural knack and sense of colour combined, always resulted in a charm of appearance, restful and attractive to the eye.

However Mistress Giles at once decided that Madame Durand was frivolous, in fact " French "; that summed up Mistress Giles' deepest disapproval.

The old lady was a good conversationalist, she had been well educated, her father having been a knight and her mother a maid of honour in Queen Elizabeth's court. This she never forgot or allowed others to forget, and that she had married beneath her when she wedded good, honest John Giles, senior, who was but a farmer, although a yeoman, possessing wide acres of his own.

Soon the little party at Heathmoor Farm was seated at a well spread table and Mistress Giles pressed the dainties on her guests, but Rachelle noticed that the children had only rye bread, a small portion of cheese and drank a very pale looking beer.

Mistress Giles ignored Rachelle in the conversation, for which she felt some relief as she still found it somewhat difficult to follow the English language, especially if spoken quickly. She noticed her neighbours took care to speak deliberately, generally raising their voices as if she were deaf, which secretly amused her, although she recognised the fact that they meant to be helpful. Mistress Giles made no effort to make herself understood by Rachelle so she gave herself up to enjoying the meal, contented herself with an occasional smile at the children and was surprised that there was no response on their faces. Lawrence the boy looked at her sullenly, while

Lovedy seemed as though any attention would make her dissolve into tears.

Mistress Giles started the talk by saying doubtless M. Durand was glad to find himself in England, evidently feeling that it was a country vastly superior to France.

M. Durand smiled and said he was grateful for the shelter afforded and for the freedom to worship according to conscience.

Mistress Giles continued: " Not that England is what it was in my young days. The nation has become degenerate, given over to pleasure. Children are disobedient and disrespectful. No one is to be trusted from the king on his throne to my wench in the kitchen."

" Oh come, come now Madam," John Giles said. " Don't give us such a bad name to M. Durand. I hope he's finding some of us trustworthy."

" Indeed I am, Mr. Giles," Gaston hastened to say.

" I adhere to what I say John. To begin with, take the king; you know how when he came to the throne he promised to preserve the government both in church and state as it was then established by law. Those were his very words in Parliament, I read it in my paper, " The Public Intelligencer." And yet almost immediately he attended mass and is placing Roman Catholics in positions of honour. What I say is, that no man should say one thing and do the opposite. I am, M. Durand, a woman of my word and when I say a thing I keep to it, as my son and these children know well."

The old lady's lips set in a firm line. Gaston and Rachelle Durand could well believe the truth of her words.

John Giles remarked soothingly: " My mother is a reader and a student of human nature, M. Durand."

He gave both the visitors the impression that he was trying to keep Mistress Giles in a peaceful frame of mind He looked and spoke as though he lived on the edge of a volcano that might explode at any moment.

Mistress Giles positively snorted.

" Any woman who isn't a fool must be the latter, and my parents, Sir and Lady Protheroe, took care that I was the former."

She then changed the topic of conversation.

" Have you heard much of this unfortunate rebellion under that poor man Monmouth, M. Durand ? "

" Not a great deal Mistress Giles, but I did hear at one of our gatherings in the Crypt of the Cathedral of its unfortunate ending."

This seemed a safe matter on which to converse and John Giles and Gaston Durand encouraged the old lady to continue and so the meal progressed.

Before leaving, Rachelle asked Mistress Giles if she would allow her grandchildren to visit them in Canterbury.

" My boy André and my little girl Ninon would like to make their acquaintance," she said speaking slowly and carefully.

Mistress Giles pursed up her lips, " I do not know Madame if I can allow it, I do not believe in frivolity for young children. Lawrence and Lovedy are not good children, they are disinclined to work and do not like lessons. Only to-day I had to chastise Lovedy for carelessness in her tapestry work. She had several stitches running from right to left instead of from left to right. Nothing but sheer perversity on her part, but I think ten stripes with the rod will have done something towards driving out that bad spirit in her. She will be more careful another time."

They were standing in the hall at the moment and Lawrence, with a scowl on his face, drew near his sister and put his arm around her.

" Lawrence," said the grandmother," do not think that I do not observe your action. I will not have Lovedy petted. I shall punish you both if I see anything more like that."

Then turning to Rachelle she said: "What children need is discipline, I expect you find that is so with your young people. I tell Lawrence and Lovedy that one day they may have a stepmother then they will surely know what real correction is. I am afraid I cannot permit them at present to accept your invitation. When I see an improvement in their conduct I might consider it."

To Mistress Giles' amazement, her son usually so submissive to her decisions spoke up: "Come, come, Madame, I should like the children to know M. and Madame Durand's young people, they are nice children."

"That's more than you can say of your own," the old lady retorted furious at her son's interference.

But John ignored her and speaking to Rachelle he said: "Thank you Madame, if you will name a day I will bring them in."

Rachelle Durand flushed. She hated being present at this family disagreement, but her husband said quickly: "What about next Saturday Mr. Giles? André has a holiday from lessons that afternoon."

So it was settled, and as the Durands left Rachelle said: "Those poor children, my heart aches for them."

Mistress Giles was too astonished to argue with her son. She ordered Lawrence and Lovedy to bed at once and went off to her own room muttering to herself: "There is some queer influence over John with those people from Canterbury. I've noticed a change in him since he started visiting them. I must do something about it. I won't stand any nonsense with my own son."

She was exceedingly angry. A strong willed woman, spoilt by an indulgent husband, left a widow, when her son was young, with control of the property, she had grown more and more tyrannical, till now she could not bear the slightest opposition from anyone.

Chapter XVI

CAPTAIN HOPKINS' VISIT

THE Durand family often spoke of Captain Hopkins, ever mindful of the kindness they had received at his hands and the pleasant days they had spent with his good wife and family. They had liked the rosy boys and girls. They had met them all, except the eldest lad of whom Captain Hopkins had loved to talk. The Durands hoped that one day they would receive a visit from the Captain as he sometimes brought his boat into Dover with a cargo and had promised when doing so, to come on to Canterbury and visit the immigrants. So they were not surprised one Summer day, when they had been in England over a year, to hear the Captain's hearty voice at the door.

He received a warm welcome and was delighted to find the Durands prospering. It was just eleven o'clock and therefore dinner time for ordinary folk when the Captain arrived, so he joined the family at the table. Fashionable people in London dined as late as one o'clock but middle class people were earlier.

Both Gaston and Rachelle noticed a difference in the Captain. He was as kindly as ever, but there was a grave look in his eyes and his laugh was less ready. He looked as though he had gone through some sad experience and when the meal was over, André gone to school, and Leonie and Ninon with M. Perrier in another room, they sat down to talk and found out that what they had conjectured was indeed so.

Rachelle inquired for Mistress Hopkins and the Captain sighed.

"She is but sadly, I am sorry to tell you. The leech tells me there is nothing really wrong with her, but she has grieved so about our eldest boy, that it has made her ill."

He paused and Gaston said: "The lad that was so clever. I am sorry indeed if anything has gone wrong with him."

Captain Hopkins placed his hand over his eyes a moment to hide a tear that glistened there.

"It's a sad story but I would like to tell you. Ah maybe, I was too proud of the boy. He took after my ancestor, Richard Woodman, who I told you was martyred for the faith, he was a man of great learning and when he died left much writing behind him. These papers were printed by one John Foxe who wrote books giving an account of the Protestant martyrs under Queen Mary. Well my boy was just as bookish. Ah! if he had kept to his books all might have been well, but he was fired by a desire to help England to be Protestant and when the Duke of Monmouth landed here last Summer meaning to wrest the crown from the king, my boy Richard, with many another young one, must needs join the rebel army. You have heard may be of its fate."

"Yes," Gaston assented and waited.

"My boy was in the battle of Sedgemoor, an army composed largely of peasants against trained men, true some of them had served in the Militia and had thus acquired some rudimentary knowledge of drill, but many were raw recruits. The king's troops were led by officers, the rebels by men without knowledge but with much religious zeal. In spite of their handicaps these men were so brave, they held their own for more than an hour on the battlefield."

The Captain paused and Rachelle said softly: "And your boy fell on the battlefield?"

"No, no, would that he had. He was taken prisoner and tried by that brute in human form, Judge Jeffreys. I cannot bring myself to speak of what the boy had to endure. We heard it all from a comrade of his who escaped. Disguised as a girl, he lingered in the neighbourhood to know my lad's fate. The woman who helped my boy's friend and gave the disguise was beheaded for what she had done. And my son! His mangled body, with that of many others, was nailed to the wall of a public building to strike terror into the hearts of all who might be tempted to rebellion. My boy was only eighteen the day he left us with such high hopes and with the one desire to help England, to enable her to serve God according to the truth."

"You have our deepest sympathy, my friend. You know that, but words are so poor to show what we feel," Gaston said.

"Thank you sir," the Captain said simply. "But one thing I know these poor men, lads, eh, and women also who suffered, did not die in vain."

Captain Hopkins lowered his voice, as if afraid to utter his thoughts. "I have recently been in Holland. I took a cargo to Amsterdam and I had converse with several men there. England is not going to submit to a Roman Catholic king. He is gradually transferring all important offices, both civil and military from Protestant holders to Roman Catholic. The whole power in Ireland has been committed to Catholics."

"Yes, I understand all this, but I fail to comprehend your reference to Holland, Captain."

"Is that so? Well, the eyes of all the Protestants in England are turning to William, Prince of Orange, husband of Mary, our king's eldest daughter. She and her husband are staunch Protestants and I hear that all orders of men both in church and state are looking to the Prince for help. If he comes he will find a vast number of people ready to support him."

"Do you mean that the idea is to place William on the throne?" M. Durand asked.

"Yes, Prince William and his wife Mary."

"Oh dear! Will that not lead to disaster as Monmouth's rebellion did?" Rachelle asked.

"No Madame, I think not. It will be a different affair altogether. James has aggravated the nation beyond endurance. He has alienated the nobility and offended the church by his foolish partiality for his confessor Father Petre, now the king is without support or good advice."

The little party sat in silence for a time, then Captain Hopkins said: "I have another piece of news for you, which I feel sure will give you joy."

"Ah, what is that?" Gaston asked.

"Well Sir, do you remember the conversation we had on the boat when crossing from your country?"

"I certainly remember much connected with that voyage, not least your extreme kindness to us all."

"Tut, tut man, that was a mere trifle. Well, I couldn't put out of my mind what you said about sin. You may recall I spoke of my good deeds and how I did not consider myself much of a sinner. Mere words I assure you, for deep down in my heart I knew better. All through the dark days of our anxiety about my lad and when the sad news came through to us of his death, I knew God was speaking to my heart. Words of Holy Writ kept coming to my mind, you see I was brought up by my good mother to know the Bible. A fine thing that is for all young people I say, it's a seed sown in the heart that will spring up some time. One day I was feeling pretty sick of myself and stricken for my loss, and I thought to myself I'm forsaken of God. I took my Bible, the very copy that my ancestor Richard Woodman treasured and I turned—it seemed by accident—to a chapter in Isaiah and read, 'Your iniquities have separated you and your God, your sins have hid His face from you.' Then as I sat turning the pages, I found another word spoken of Israel, 'She drew not near to her God.' I remembered the story of the prodigal son, it was not the father's fault that the son was in the far country, it was the son who had withdrawn himself from the father. I recalled the words, 'Draw nigh to God and He will draw nigh to you.' I fell on my knees and cried, 'How can I, a helpless sinner, draw nigh to God ?' Immediately the words came to me, 'Made nigh by the Blood of Christ.' The words fell on my troubled spirit like a healing balm. Because of that shed Blood, that Life poured forth, I, a worthless sinner, could draw nigh to God. I thanked God for His Son Who so freely gave Himself for me, and I knew His salvation had come to my heart."

"Thank God," Gaston and Rachelle both said.

The Captain's visit was but brief, he had to rejoin his ship, he went off promising to come again one day. In spite of his sad loss the Durands knew that the Captain was a happier man than when they saw him last. Graver certainly, but there was a peaceful look in his eyes, which spoke silently, but eloquently, of rest of heart.

CHAPTER XVII

LAWRENCE

THE next event in the Durand family was the arrival on the following day of Lawrence and Lovedy Giles. Their father brought them and said he had business in the town and would come for them later. He felt that his boy and girl would make friends more easily with the young people without restraint of his presence. His mother was constantly warning him that any kindness he might show to his children was spoiling them and unfitting them to bear the trials of life that would surely come later, so he had often checked some gentle impulse which had come to him, and now a barrier had grown up between himself and the children. A barrier, that now John Giles had seen the happy home atmosphere in the Durand household, he regretted sincerely. Naturally a shy man, always repressed from childhood by his mother, he felt unable to do or say anything to show the real affection he felt for his son and daughter.

However, it was a step in the right direction that he had been firm in accepting the invitation for them from the Durands, in spite of the grandmother's opposition.

It seemed at first that Lovedy and Lawrence were going to be difficult children to entertain, silently they sat on the chairs Madame Durand placed for them. Leonie eyed them with an unblushing stare, but to Madame's surprise Ninon came forward, saying to Lovedy: " Would you like to see my St. Bartholomew baby ? * She is such

* Dolls were sold in the fairs on St. Bartholomew's Day, hence the name.

a beauty, and she has a gown that I made for her myself."

The fact was Ninon had felt a wave of pity for the forlorn looking little girl. She herself wore a pretty frock of blue taffeta, her hair was curled, while poor Lovedy's dress was of linsey-woolsey of the colour known as "sad," while her hair was brushed back and kept in place by a coarse net.

Madame Durand decided to leave the little girls alone, knowing that children make friends better without the supervision of a grown up person.

André took Lawrence to see the looms. Presently he sought his Aunt saying: "Aunt Marie, I'm sure Lawrence is ill, he looks so white and he says his head aches. Do you know that horrid old grandmother boxed his ears so roughly, just before he came away, that it has made him very queer."

"Poor lad," Marie said and followed André to the workroom where Lawrence sat holding his head.

"Come with me, Lawrence," Marie said gently and took him to her room where she made him lie down on a couch, covering him with a rug and putting a cushion under his head.

"Now just lie still and keep your eyes shut," she said.

She left him for a few moments returning with a bowl of hot water. Placing it on a chair, she then proceeded to immerse a soft cloth in the water, next wringing it out, and then gently bathing the boy's forehead with firm strokes, over and over again she reheated the cloth and continued the bathing. Once or twice Lawrence murmured: "Thank you." After a time Marie saw that he had fallen asleep, so soothing had been her ministration. He did not doze long but as he began to wake, he looked up at Marie and said, still half asleep: "Oh you are lovely!"

Then he became wholly awake and sat up saying

apologetically: " I am giving you a lot of trouble."

" Not at all my dear, I am so glad to help anyone who is in need. No, don't sit up, you must lie still. Is the head better ? "

" Much better, thank you."

" But not quite well, so you must not join the others yet or it may come back again. I am going to bring you a cup of the new China drink. I found it most refreshing the other day when I wasn't well."

Lawrence lay back with a sigh of satisfaction. It was so delightful to be taken care of like this, such a new experience. Why it would be well worth while being ill to be nursed by Aunt Marie. It reminded him of something that was just a faint memory, the time long ago when his mother had been alive and he had sat on her lap. But he had been only a little four-year-old when she died, so the remembrance was but faint.

That evening when John Giles called for his children, he stood in the doorway of the living room watching a merry scene. Gaston Durand had suggested a game of blind man's buff. At the moment when John stood looking in, Gaston Durand had just caught Lovedy, who with shouts of merriment was returning a bear's hug. Suddenly she caught sight of her father and at once her laughter ceased, and she struggled away from M. Durand's arms, and was once again the demure, little maiden that her father knew so well.

The swift change of demeanour brought a sudden pang to the father's heart, and he determined to do his utmost to break down this barrier of reserve and fear that evidently existed in his daughter's heart, so on the way home he exerted himself to talk to the children asking them questions about their visit and encouraging them to give him their confidence. Lovedy was riding a pony, while Lawrence and her father walked beside her. John was delighted to find his son and daughter responded to his advances. The happy time they had had with the Durands had stirred them out of their usual apathy and they chatted freely. Lovedy announcing: "Ninon has promised to be my special friend for ever and ever," while Lawrence said: "She is such a kind girl, but Mademoiselle Marie is an angel."

When they arrived home their grandmother was watching from a window. A dark frown settled on her face as she noted the evidence of cheerful comradeship between her son and his children. Lovedy's bright face and Lawrence's voice in conversation did not escape her notice. She was annoyed. The fact was, although John would have been amazed to know it, she was passionately attached to her son, and possessing a grasping, jealous disposition could not bear to see him giving attention to any other object than herself. She craved his love, but did not see that her attitude to him and the children destroyed the very thing she ardently desired.

Now she received the little group with cold words and colder looks. In the days that followed she vented her spite and jealousy on the poor children in many petty ways. She was not slow to see that John invented excuses for visiting Canterbury and she said more than once to the children: "In my opinion it will not be long before you have a stepmother and then you will learn what discipline really is like. Stepmothers are always cruel and she will make your father hate you."

The words struck terror to the children's hearts. From whence the dreaded stepmother was to come, they had no idea. Lawrence's face grew more sullen and Lovedy seemed to be perpetually in tears.

John Giles said to himself: "I cannot let things go on like this. I must take action, but—but will she be willing? How can I, a stodgy farmer hope to win so finely made, so beautiful a woman?"

Chapter XVIII

CATHERINE'S PLAN

CATHERINE de VERE grew more and more excited as the day grew near for her to leave the convent school and go home, but she did not forget her determination to rescue the girl, who had attracted her notice, she was quite strong in her purpose to secure her services as a maid.

Catherine had always been greatly indulged by her father and brother, and was also a pet with the Abbess. Of a singularly sunny disposition, naturally unselfish, she had not been spoilt by all the good things she had received in life, although it has certainly made her fairly persistent in getting her own way; that her way was generally some kind, gracious scheme was a happy coincidence.

For the prisoners in the dungeons the days seemed long and monotonous and when one by one they were released for examination, the Abbess found, in one or two cases, her method had been successful from her point of view, her victims yielded to her dictates and professed themselves willing to go to mass and accept the religion of the king. To their dismay they found that this did not secure freedom, they were to remain as servants in the convents, and bitter were their thoughts and tears, as they realised they had denied their Saviour and obtained no material, earthly good by so doing. Others stood firm and were subjected to harder treatment.

When Jacqueline Goyer's turn came for examination although trembling in every limb, she had such a sense of the overshadowing, protecting Presence of her Lord, that she was prepared to stand firm for Him, but the physical strain through which she had passed, the scanty food, the long hours in the badly ventilated cell had so weakened her not too strong body, that instead of answering the Abbess' question she sunk on the floor in a dead faint.

The Abbess frowned. She turned to a nun standing by and said: " Take her away."

Now the nun addressed was a kindly-hearted woman and instead of carrying Jacqueline to the gloomy dungeon, she carried the helpless girl to her own cell and cared for her until she revived. Then the nun hastened to the kitchen and coaxed from the cook a bowl of nourishing soup.

How delicious it tasted to poor famished Jacqueline after weeks of semi-starvation. A faint colour came back into her face as she sipped it.

" There child, you lie still and keep quiet. I don't know what the Abbess will wish for you, but anyhow until we know, you might as well rest here," the rosy-cheeked kind nun said.

She then left Jacqueline alone, who was only too thankful to lie still and thank God that there were still some kind hearts left in the world.

The nun as she left the cell, omitted to shut the door, so it happened that, presently, Stephanie Legier was doing what she had no right to do, prowling around in the nuns' quarters. Seeing a door ajar, with her usual curiosity, she peeped in and stared in with amazement at Jacqueline as she lay on the bed.

" Why that's the girl that is so like Catherine. I'll run and tell her. It's recess time so Catherine can come and look at her."

Jacqueline's eyes were closed, so she had no idea that any one was peeping curiously at her. Stephanie, bubbling over with delight that she had an unusual bit of news for Catherine, soon found her friend and told her what she had discovered.

" Do come and peep at her. You will see how much she is like you."

Catherine did not hesitate, although she knew they were both breaking rules. Together they hurried to the cell and Catherine entered, while Stephanie kept watch at the door.

Catherine exclaimed under her breath. The look on Jacqueline's face amazed her. The girl lay so white and still, thin to the point of emaciation, yet her countenance gave an impression of peace, almost of joy, as Catherine stood there watching her. If Catherine had known Jacqueline's thoughts probably they would not have solved the puzzle of the girl's calm face, for Catherine was a stranger to God. As Jacqueline lay on the nun's couch her mind had been filled with the thought of God's care for her, and she had the assurance that He was planning for her future. There had been hours of haunting dread and sickening terror, in which Jacqueline could only cry: " O God help me, help me." Help had come and now although she knew not what was ahead of her, yet in faith she murmured: " Thank You Father, I know all will be well."

Then she opened her eyes and saw the bright, young face bending over her. She was still a bit dazed from her fainting attack and she said in a tone of bewilderment: " Oh has He sent an angel ? "

Catherine laughed merrily.

" No, not an angel, you poor girl, but a friend. Listen I can only stay a moment. I am leaving here next week and I want to take you with me. Will you be my maid ? "

Jacqueline was now sitting up, fully conscious of what was happening.

" Oh dear lady, I will gladly go anywhere with you.

Can you really take me away from this dreadful place ? "

" I hope so, I'll try hard. Tell me your name."

Jacqueline told her and at that moment Stephanie whispered: " Come Catherine, come, I hear someone coming. We must go."

Together the girls fled back to the schoolroom.

Stephanie and Catherine had many a conversation as how best to get Jacqueline away. Stephanie was all for some disguise, some plot to outwit the Abbess, intrigue she loved, and she made many suggestions, some wild, others fairly practicable. But Catherine determined first to try a straightforward method, and at a favourable moment approach the Abbess. She asked for an interview and her request was granted. First she diplomatically thanked the Abbess for all her kindness to her during her stay in the Convent. The Abbess was pleased and smiled benignly at her favourite pupil.

" You have always been a docile child and I shall have a good report to send to your father. I could have wished that you had had a vocation, but your parent has decreed otherwise."

" Yes mother that is so, but possibly I shall be able to serve the church in the world."

" Perhaps so, but not my child in the same way or to such a degree as in a convent."

Catherine spoke eagerly.

" Mother, I am thinking if you will give me your permission, I see a way in which I can serve the church."

" You do, my daughter. Explain yourself."

" If you would allow me to take that girl Jacqueline Goyer away with me, I will do my best to convert her to the true faith. I think severity will never accomplish that with her, but if I am kind to her and she gets fond of me, she will yield to my wishes. That will be a good deed and a service to the church, will it not, mother ? "

"And may I inquire how you know anything about this girl, her name for instance?"

The Abbess spoke stiffly.

"Two days ago, Sister Marie Agathe sent Jacqueline into the garden to hang out some laundry, it was recess time and I was walking in the garden and I took the opportunity of speaking to the girl. I liked her and it seemed to me such a pity that she should be a heretic."

"Very remiss of you, Catherine, you should not have spoken to one who is so sinful."

Catherine's face fell, but the Abbess added: "There, no doubt you meant well and I hope you will always be so zealous to win souls from the pathway of error into the true fold. But if I consent to your taking this girl, what will your father say?"

"Father won't mind, mother. He will be pleased for me to have her as my maid and win her back to the faith."

The Abbess sat deep in thought awhile and then she said: "Very well Catherine, you may have Jacqueline on one condition. I give you twelve months and if at the end of that time she is not a convert, she must be sent back here and I shall spare no discipline in order to reclaim her. If fair means have failed then it must be severity. I fear it is very lax of me to let you try this easy way first. I should convert her and then send her to you."

"Oh no, mother. Please let me try. I feel sure I shall succeed."

"Just one year then, no longer, unless you have made her recant."

One year! It seemed a short period, but much can happen in a year. Could the Abbess have foreseen what would occur, Catherine's request would have been emphatically denied.

Two days later when Jacqueline awoke from her sleep,

she found a complete set of new clothing by her bed, including a travelling cloak and hood. She dressed wonderingly, and had only just completed her attire when Sister Marie Agathe came bustling in.

"You are dressed, that's right. Come and have some breakfast. The coach will be at the door in half-an-hour. Mademoiselle de Vere's trunks are in the hall ready for the start."

"Oh-h! Am I really going with her?"

"Of course. I thought you knew. That is why you have new clothes. If you are to be a maid you must be suitably attired and the things you wore over a month in that dungeon are only fit for the fire."

Jacqueline could scarcely eat her breakfast for joy. A mixture of fear and joy, joy at the prospect before her, fear, that at the last moment the Abbess should change her mind and withhold her permission for the departure.

But all went well and soon Catherine and Jacqueline, accompanied by a dour-faced nun, were off. Jacqueline sat quietly in her corner of the coach and Catherine, although bubbling over with excitement, managed to restrain her feelings as long as the nun was with them, the girls thought her hard and cold, how little they knew that every step of that journey meant pain to the nun, for it was full of memories of a happy girlhood, before hope and joy had died out of her life.

When at noon they stopped at a wayside inn and were met there by M. de Vere with his own coach and servants, Catherine said farewell to the nun and exclaimed delightedly: "There, now I'm finished with the convent school for ever and ever. Oh father, isn't it glorious? I'm home for good now."

M. de Vere patted his daughter's shoulder. "You are not more pleased than I am, my dear. Come, now we must get a meal while the horses feed and then turn our faces homeward. And who have you here my child? Is she your maid?"

"Yes Father. This is Jacqueline Goyer, whom the Abbess allowed me to have as my maid."

"What will Nanette say?

"Oh Nanette is getting too old. She must rest now. I like someone young about me."

M. de Vere smiled and turning to Jacqueline said: "Well Goyer, I hope you will be happy with us. I like everybody around me to be so."

Jacqueline flushed and made a curtsey, murmuring: "Thank you, Monsieur."

Chapter XIX

CATHERINE'S ARGUMENTS

JACQUELINE was not disappointed as she grew more acquainted with her young mistress. She found Catherine kind and considerate, waiting on her was a delight to Jacqueline. The château of M. de Vere was a haven of rest to the poor girl, she thought of herself as a battered storm-tossed ship that had found a temporary harbour. She tried to live in the present, but it was not easy, her thoughts went frequently back to the old days at home, and her dear mother. She longed to know what had become of her father and Pierre Benoit. She dared not let herself look forward, a year would soon pass and then she was to be returned to the convent with the certainty that severe persecution awaited her.

Over and over she whispered to herself the words of the text: "He hath said, 'I will never leave thee, nor forsake thee,' so that we may boldly say 'I will not fear what man shall do unto me.'"

But she could not but be grave, her past suffering had left a mark on the girl, her present anxiety as to the fate of the two she loved best, and the uncertainty of her future combined to check the natural gaiety of youth. Notwithstanding there was a quiet peace about her, that sometimes made Catherine de Vere look at her in a puzzled fashion.

One day when the two had been together about a month, Catherine said: "Look here Jacqueline, it's time I set to work to convert you. I promised the Abbess I would accomplish it in a year, so I had better make a start. Fancy I've been home a month, it seems like a day or two the time goes so quickly and so merrily. But this morning I'm not riding with father, the poor dear's gouty foot is troubling him, so you and I will take our needlework into the garden and I will set to work to show you the error of your way."

Catherine laughed gaily.

"Behold me, a father confessor, a mother superior, doctor of religion, priest, friar, and what not, all rolled together. But there, you dear, gentle soul, I know you will do what I wish, come along, bring the work basket."

The two were soon seated in a shady corner under a spreading tree, in front of them lay a wide stretch of garden, bright with late summer flowers, beyond that parkland dotted here and there with trees, in the far distance a line of blue hills. Close to them a peacock flaunted his beauty and a few doves cooed from a columnbarium. All spoke of peace and it was difficult to realise that not far off, men and women were suffering for the faith, some in dungeons, some disguised in various ways seeking to escape from their fatherland, ruled by a king so blinded to the best interest of his country, so bigoted, that he would lose his most worthy subjects rather than permit religious freedom.

Catherine made herself comfortable with a supply of cushions and settled down prepared for a long talk.

"Now Jacqueline tell me all about yourself first. I only know your mother was killed, but had you no other relations ?"

"Yes Mademoiselle, my father. I don't know what has become of him, I fear he too was killed or he would have sought me ere this."

"Or he might have been sent to the galleys. My brother told me that was the fate of many of the men."

Jacqueline's face grew pale and her hands trembled. She had heard much of the horrible life of the galley slaves.

Catherine noticed her agitation and hastened to say: " Perhaps I am wrong. We will hope he is all right and will find you some day. Was there anyone else ? "

" Yes, my lover, Pierre Benoit," Jacqueline said simply.

" Oh, how interesting ! You really had a lover. I wish we could find him. Poor Jacqueline. I'm so sorry for you, no wonder you look so—well not exactly sad, but grave. Now what I cannot understand is, why your people and hundreds of others should so cling to what is just an idea really, and be willing to suffer for it. Mind you I don't approve of this religious persecution. I think everybody should be allowed to think what they please. I should like to make every one happy. But suffer and lose for the sake of a religion ! It isn't worth it. If it pleases the king, or my father or his chaplain for me to go to mass or confession occasionally, well, it does me no harm, I don't believe it does me any good, but certainly I should never think it worth while to make myself, or any one unhappy by refusing to oblige in such a trifling matter. You will be docile, won't you Jacqueline, and come to mass with me ? Then I can send a message to the Abbess and say all is well. We will also send your name to the king's minister, the Marquis de Louvois, and all be settled. The Marquis is very keen on adding names to his list of converts. He boasts that he has made sixty thousand conversions in the district of Bordeaux, that brings him into favour with the king, so my brother tells me."

Jacqueline spoke very quietly.

" I am sorry Mademoiselle, you know I would do almost anything for you, you have done so much for me, but there is One Who has done far more, He died for me and I cannot deny Him."

" Of Whom are you talking Jacqueline ? "

" The Lord Jesus Christ, Mademoiselle."

" Oh the Christ ! But that was so long ago and don't

you think you are rather presumptuous to say He died for you, just an ordinary girl. You speak as though the Christ was or is a Reality to you, as though you matter to Him."

Jacqueline's eyes shone.

"He is real to me. When I was shut up in that dungeon and the darkness seemed so terrible, I was conscious of His Presence, although the actual gloom was still there of course, I became indifferent to it. I used to whisper 'Jesus my Saviour is here. He is my Light.'"

"But Jacqueline, wasn't that just imagination? What ground have you for such an idea? Could you prove that Christ was with you?"

"Yes Mademoiselle. As I believed the words of Scripture which says, 'I will never leave thee nor forsake thee,' my heart was filled with the sense of His Presence. He was real to me. He said too, 'When thou passest through the waters I will be with thee,' the Saviour keeps His word. Another text tells us we may look at the things which are not seen with our physical eyes but with the eyes of faith."

"Jacqueline, you surprise me, I thought you were a simple, uneducated, peasant girl, you talk like—like a great teacher or a philosopher. How do you know so much?"

"I think Mademoiselle, that during that month in the dungeon, God's Holy Spirit taught me many things. Of course I had always had the advantage of teaching in our Huguenots' gatherings, from the Bible, but it has been more real to me since my trial."

"God's Holy Spirit teaches you," Catherine repeated wonderingly. "Do you think He would teach me?"

Then she laughed and shrugged her shoulders.

"Dear me, what am I saying. I must not let you make me gloomy, I am too full of life and joy to want too much religion yet. When one is old it may be different."

"The young sometimes die," Jacqueline said simply.

Catherine gave a little scream and put both her hands over her ears.

"Really Jacqueline you are too terrible. Don't let me hear you speak of—of such a thing again. It is the one thing I always try to forget. I shall be cross with you if you remind me of it. I hate even to say the word 'death.' Now let us be practical. Will you come with me to mass to-morrow morning?"

Jacqueline's reply was low but firm.

"No, Mademoiselle."

"But why?"

"Mademoiselle you worship that little wafer that the priest exalts, you say it is literally the Christ. To me that is idolatry. It is still only flour and water."

Catherine again screamed.

"My dear girl you are too literal. Do not go into such details. We must please the king and the priest. And perhaps a little religion may be a help when—when —you know what I mean."

"Not religion Mademoiselle. Christ the Saviour is the One Who can help in the hour of death."

Catherine jumped.

"Jacqueline you are hopeless. I won't talk to you any longer. Come let us gather flowers and decorate the hall and the drawing-room. Did I tell you my brother Capitaine de Vere may be at home to-night?"

Chapter XX

RENE DE VERE

CAPITAINE RENE de VERE arrived home a few hours after Catherine and Jacqueline's conversation. In the days that followed Jacqueline was left to her resources, she found plenty of occupation in mending a quantity of old lace which had belonged to Catherine's mother and which she now wished to make use of on her evening dresses. While Jacqueline sat at her work her thoughts were busy. It pained her to refuse her young mistress' request, for Catherine had shown Jacqueline much kindness. The outlook for the future could not but look forbidding, but in spite of this there was trust in Jacqueline's heart.

"God will undertake for me, I am sure," she said to herself many times.

Then she prayed for her mistress, that the Light might come to her soul, she prayed for her father and Pierre wherever they might be, that they too might be comforted, as she herself was. The work of grace in Jacqueline's heart was deepening daily as she learnt more of her Saviour's power to keep, and the quiet times of communion with Him were precious, so she was not sorry to be alone.

Catherine was delighted to have her brother at home and they had a few gay days, but Catherine noticed that more than once René seemed sad and absent minded. On the last evening of his leave, she began talking about Jacqueline and told René of Jacqueline's anxiety about her father and sweetheart.

"I may be able to tell you what became of them,"

René said. " I have a list of the names of the men who were sent to the galleys. I will look it up for you."

He rang a bell and when his valet appeared sent him to bring a dispatch box. When it was brought René opened it, and taking out a number of papers studied them.

" Yes, here it is. What are the names you want ? "

" Jacqueline's surname is Goyer and her sweetheart's name is Pierre Benoit."

' H-m-m ! " René looked down the list. " Yes, Pierre Benoit and Jacques Goyer, both sent to the galleys. Poor girl she'll never see either again I fear."

" I don't think I'll tell her. Perhaps if nothing is said, she will forget them. I must try and get her another lover," Catherine remarked. " But René isn't it tiresome ? The Abbess only lets me have Jacqueline for twelve months, if at the end of that time I have not made her a Papist, she has to go back to the Convent."

" Well can't you convert her ? "

" No. I believe she is more likely to convert me. Of course I don't really mean that, but honestly René, there is something very attractive about her religion. In spite of her sorrows she has a strange peace. She says it is the peace of God in her heart and she knows the Presence of the Saviour with her. Sometimes I find myself wishing I were like her."

René started.

" Do you really feel like that, little sister ? I am feeling the same. My dealings with those poor persecuted Huguenots has convinced me that they, not we, have the true religion. The other day I stood by and saw an old man die through wounds he had received from my men. I naturally expected him to curse me and my men, but he prayed for us and when a priest said to him ' Confess, confess your sins ere it be too late,' he answered, ' I have confessed to my Saviour, I have His forgiveness, I am cleansed through His Blood, saved by His death.' The priest said something about purgatory and hell, and the old man said, 'There is no condemnation for me, Christ bore the judgment my sins deserved.' Then he grew weaker, but his face shone and he said, quite distinctly, with his dying breath, 'Saviour Thou hast come for me.' A death like that makes one think furiously."

Catherine was grave.

"René I hate the thought of death. I dread purgatory. I try not to think of it, but Jacqueline said the other day, 'The young sometimes die.' I scolded her and told her never to say such a thing again, but I cannot forget it. If one could only feel safe like those Huguenots seem to do."

René was turning out his case and presently he produced a book.

"Look Catherine. This is a Huguenot Bible, part of it I think. As it is called 'The New Testament.' I suppose there must be a part called 'The Old.' I took this from a house where the inhabitants had fled. I have been studying it and I cannot find one mention of purgatory, not much about the Virgin Mary, certainly there are no directions to worship her or pray to her. I find that the Lord Jesus said, 'Come unto Me.' He did not say approach me through the Virgin nor any saint."

"Do let me read those words," Catherine said eagerly.

"Here they are. I like them so much that I put a marker in the place."

Catherine read slowly.

"Come unto Me all ye that labour and are heavy laden and I will give you rest."

Her eyes filled with tears and she was silent.

Presently she said: "René I feel pulled two ways. This new religion appeals to me somehow. It seems to tug at my heart, but on the other hand I feel it would cost too much. I could never stand persecution, I simply couldn't and you dearest, for you it would mean disgrace."

"It would mean death," René said gravely. "Perhaps we had better forget all about it, little sister."

And Catherine agreed that it was wisest to do so.

Chapter XXI

THE DECISION

RENE de VERE walked alone in the woods. It was Springtime, he had been away from home the whole of the Winter and it had been a time of mental torture to him.

The king, Louis XIV had shewn increasing hatred to the Huguenots. His Jesuit confessor, Pere la Chaise and his new queen (Madame de Maintenon) fanned the flame of his fire. The Edict of Nantes promulgated in 1598, wherein comparative liberty of conscience and freedom of worship had been given was now revoked. Of that Edict Pope Clement VIII wrote: " A decree which gave liberty of conscience to all, was the most cursed ever made." * But now these years of liberty had passed and edict after edict came into force, each one more severe than the last. The Protestant churches were levelled to the ground, eight hundred falling in a few weeks. Children were torn from their mother's arms and placed in convents, men young and old, even boys, were sent to the galleys, women were imprisoned for life.

René de Vere who witnessed scene after scene of suffering, had, in fact, been obliged to take part in it all, in virtue of his position as an officer in the king's army and his whole soul was sickened with what he had seen and heard.

Now he was once again home on leave, a long leave this time, for the medical officer of his corps had declared him at the moment as unfit for active service. Alone in the wood René sat down on a fallen log and gave himself

* See SMILES' *Huguenots.*

up to thought. His mind went back over some of the happenings of the past months. He recalled how he had stood by, when the gallant Admiral Duquesne, the first sailor of France and a Huguenot, had replied to the king when he urged the Admiral to abjure his religion: "For sixty years, Sire, have I rendered to Cæsar the things which are Cæsar's; suffer me still to render unto God the things which are God's."

With this speech he pointed to his white hair for he was eighty years of age.

René visualised another scene.

A party of Huguenots had started for Holland, but alas, were captured and in order to intimidate any who might be contemplating flight, they were led through several principal towns as a show, with heavy chains round their necks, in some cases the chains weighing fifty pounds. They were forced to make long marches driven on with hard blows and then they were finally sent to the galleys.

What had lingered in René's mind was the expression on the faces of these captured men. He would have expected them to show signs of terror, but no; fatigue was there, sometimes blood, from the cruel whips, but a quiet look of peace, even of triumph characterised the majority. They had the air of conquerors, and René became more and more convinced that the Huguenots were upheld by a power which could not be accounted for by mere human self-control.

How many times during that Winter he had contrived to connive at some escape, to look the other way when he should have been noticing some shrinking figure gliding quietly out of the town in the dusk, he himself could not have said. He began to be aware that suspicion was falling on him and that the medical officer's decision that he needed a rest was not because of physical weakness but that same officer, being a friend of his, had probably thought: "de Vere is better out of this."

That morning in the quiet wood he was determined to come to some decision. It was impossible to continue as he was. There was a sore conflict in his heart; the flesh shrank from all that it must mean should he decide for Christ, certainly disgrace and banishment from home, if not death. He thought of his old father. What would he say? His loved sister, she too seemed to have leanings towards the Protestant faith, if he drew attention to himself by denouncing the religion of his forefathers, would Catherine be involved?

René groaned. The struggle was great. Could he endure to be an outcast in a strange land, or worse than that? He took from his pocket his New Testament which he had been studying frequently. It fell open at a chapter he had read more than once. His eye caught the words spoken to Paul: "Why persecutest thou Me?" Other words came to his memory. "He that is not with Me is against Me."

It seemed to him that Christ drew near to him and in gentle tones asked: "Are you going to be on My side or against Me?"

René turned to the story of the crucifixion, and as he read, an overwhelming realisation of what Christ had suffered for sinners, like himself, broke him down completely. He fell on his knees and prayed.

"Oh God forgive me that I have so long held out against Thy pleadings, blot out my sins, save me for the sake of the Saviour Who died for me."

Long he knelt there in silence. An inquisitive robin hopped near and with bright eyes gazed at the still figure, a rabbit came out of a hole and nibbled grass at his side, but he was unconscious of them both. When at last René lifted up his face, it was tear-stained, but a new look of peace and gladness shone there. He rose slowly to his feet and wended his way back to the château determined to tell his father what had taken place at the earliest opportunity.

The chance came that evening, when darkness had fallen. M. de Vere, Catherine and René sat in the hall round a log fire.

Although it was May the evenings were chilly and the warmth of the fire was pleasant.

René sat in silence awhile taking note of the faces of his parent and sister. The father with his white hair and aristocratic countenance, his kindly eye and smile of satisfaction as he looked at his son and daughter. René's glance then fell on Catherine, she sat on a low stool near the hearth, the firelight gleamed on her white, softly rounded arms, on one shone a bracelet of gold, studded with gleaming brilliant diamonds, her face was mostly in the shadow, but now and again the flickering flames cast a light showing up the golden tints in her hair and the delicate complexion of her pink cheeks.

René said to himself: " I shall always keep this charming picture in my memory. I shall probably never see it again, but to-night will leave an indelible mark on my mind."

Presently his father spoke.

" You are quiet to-night, my son. Is it that you are not well ? "

" No Sir, I am well, but I have much on my mind. I find it difficult to tell you and I fear when I do I shall give you pain."

The old man started, but spoke quietly: " Do not be afraid my boy. Have you been getting into debt or have you had a quarrel with a fellow officer ? Tell me honestly and I shall do all I can to help you."

"Oh no sir. Nothing like that. I will come straight to the point. I am a Huguenot. I no longer belong to the Roman Catholic Church. I have found the Christ or rather He has found me."

"René, it is impossible. You are an officer in the king's army. My son is this madness? Perhaps your medical officer has detected symptoms of insanity that he has sent you home."

"No Father, I am perfectly sane I assure you. Let me try and make the matter clear to you. You know the horrible work on which I have been engaged for many months. I have seen men, women and even children shamefully treated because of their faith and never once have I heard one curse his or her fate, never once have I heard pity for themselves, rather I have seen noble actions, patient suffering, even more, triumph in the hour of death, peace in pain and prayer for the persecutors. Well Sir, this has led me to think tremendously. What could be the secret of their victory? I pondered much. Then I found a New Testament in a deserted house, I took it and have studied it, in consequence of which I feel I have heard God's Voice, His message to my soul. It has meant a new knowledge of myself. I know that I am a sinner, lost and undone apart from His saving mercy, the grace of the One Who gave His Son to die in order to make an atonement for my soul. Through Him I have life, life eternal."

René paused and his father seemed too amazed for speech. Presently he spoke: "My son, my son! Do you really mean that you have turned your back on the religion in which you have been reared?"

"Yes sir."

"Then your life will not be safe in this land."

"I fear not sir."

"René, this indeed is a blow to me. Let me think.

Nothing matters as much as your safety. We must keep this matter secret. You must pretend to be ill and remain quietly at home, even then I fear if you do not attend mass and go to confession your changed views will become known and you will be hunted out. My son, my son, truly this will bring my grey hairs in sorrow to the grave ! "

René was very moved. That his father did not denounce him or utter one word of reproach made his heart ache.

" Father, God will guide us what to do and if I am called to suffer for His sake He will strengthen me."

All through this conversation Catherine had sat silent. René wondered for it was unlike her usual rapid, active mentality. Now she spoke. " Father, I too have a confession to make. I have become a Protestant."

" My daughter ! But what has influenced you ? You have not had the same experience as your brother."

" No father. But you remember when I brought Jacqueline home from the convent I promised the Abbess to convert her in a year. The exact opposite has happened. Jacqueline has won me for the Saviour."

" Catherine my child what are you saying ? What are we to do ? I am bewildered. I know not what to say to you. Let me think, that such a thing should happen to us would seem amazing, but it is the past over again."

The old man paused, hid his face in his hands and there was a great stillness in the room. René and Catherine were puzzled by their father's remark, but neither spoke. The thoughts of all three were too deep, too poignant for easy expression.

M. de Vere was the first to speak, and his words came slowly.

" Ah it all comes back to me ! René you have some remembrance of your dear mother, but you, Catherine, were only a babe three days old when she died. My wife, my beautiful Louise ! I never told you, for I tried to forget, she died a Protestant, she refused the last rites of the church. She begged me to read the Bible and teach you two the truth, as she called it. But I locked her Bible away and let you be taught by Pére Moisseau. Ah ! my wife with her dying breath commended you both to her Saviour, for that was how she spoke of the Christ."

"This is indeed wonderful news, sir. Then the fact that Catherine and I have both learnt the truth and accepted it, is an answer to our mother's prayer for us."

"Yes it must be so. In spite of my disregard of my dear Louise' wish, God has fulfilled her desire. Tell me Catherine was it only the influence of that simple girl that decided you ?"

"René lent me his copy of the Testament for a few days when last he was at home. When I showed it to Jacqueline, she said: 'That is God's message to us.' I replied, 'Well, if God has sent us a message surely we ought to know something about it.' So I read the Book. One night I read right on to the dawn and was greatly impressed. Then René left and took the Book with him, but I found that Jacqueline, although she cannot read, yet knew many portions by heart. She has been taught from childhood by a pastor of the little church where her parents worshipped. The words repeated to me by Jacqueline entered my heart and I too want to confess that I belong to Christ. Father, I cannot go any more to mass and confession. I cannot worship the host. Christ is not in that little wafer, it is idolatrous to worship it, for it is only a symbol."

Old M. de Vere looked suddenly aged and stricken, only too well he realised what this might mean for his son and daughter.

"What can I say?" he repeated. "What can I do? How can I shelter you both?"

The three sat in silence for a moment or two. Catherine was holding her father's hand and stroking it gently. Both she and René were praying for guidance. Suddenly Catherine exclaimed: "Father no one knows anything of this, would it not be wise for René and me to leave France before it becomes known. Our neighbours know that René is home on sick leave, they would think he was travelling for his health. Let us go off quite openly and get to— to— well somewhere."

"Holland," René added. "I could join the army of the Prince of Orange. I hear that several Huguenot officers have done that."

"I think Catherine's suggestion is a good one," M. de Vere said sadly.

"But you will come with us Father, won't you?" Catherine asked.

"No my dear, I think not. I am old. I am still a Catholic. I must stay here and see to my estate. I can then keep you well supplied with funds. Alas, alas! My old age will be desolate, but your safety is more to me than my own comfort. My children, my children!"

Catherine burst into tears and clung to her father sobbing. René's eyes were by no means dry. It was a sad moment. M. de Vere was the first to recover calmness.

"My dears, you had better pack to-night and be off in the morning. Our coach will take you the first stage of your journey, after that you must hire. I have plenty of gold in the house and can supply you. Then when you have reached Holland and have a settled address I can communicate with you."

"Father, you are wonderful, noble indeed. Not one word of reproach, and you are willing to sacrifice for us," René said brokenly.

" My children I love you," the old man replied simply.

" Father, I have my papers for resignation here, foreseeing that I should have to resign my commission. I will sign them and leave them with you and when you hear we are safely in Holland you can send them in."

" Oh Father if only you would come with us, I should not mind," Catherine said again.

" My child I can best serve you by remaining here for the present, if later I can sell all, then I can join you. I will then have the price of my land to invest in England. I am too old to change my religion, but although I must still remain a Catholic, I intend reading my wife's Bible. I suppose no one will hinder my doing that."

" I don't know sir. Liberty has gone from our land. France is turning out or killing all those who honour God. There will presently be a nation of atheists, for no thinking man can accept the travesty of religion offered by the priests. Religion, as represented by the leaders of the Catholic party, will fall into contempt."

" Alas, my son I fear you are right."

Jacqueline was amazed when Catherine told her they were to pack in haste that evening. She was delighted to find they were going to leave France, for the thought of returning to the convent at the end of the year had never been long out of her mind.

It was a sad parting the next morning. In the seclusion of the breakfast room Catherine clung to her father and René stood by with white drawn face. It was here the real " good-bye " must be said, for in the sight of the servants at the hall door, where the huge family coach was drawn up, the farewell must appear to be a lighthearted one. It must look as though the separation was only for a short time while Catherine and René were travelling for change and pleasure. It was not easy to assume cheerfulness when their hearts were well nigh breaking, but it was done. Catherine waved and smiled as her father called out: " Au revoir."

Would they ever see him again? It was doubtful. And so they were off.

Travelling in style, an officer of the king's army, was everywhere treated with respect, so eventually they found themselves safely in Holland and were welcomed by some fellow countrymen who had already found a haven there.

Chapter XXII

THE STEPMOTHER

MARIE DURAND was deep in thought. It was true her hands were engaged with some knitting, but it was work that did not need any particular attention on her part, and as she sat at work, she pondered. She went back over the time when she and her relations had left France, how great had been her sorrow then, for although Marie was quiet and had kept up a show of cheerful acquiescence to the circumstances for the sake of the others, yet it had been a time of heart break for her. Naturally rather timid she had shrunk from the unknown, but her trust had been in God. How often had she found comfort in the thought of Abram of old, who had gone out, "Not knowing whither he went," and how God had protected and led him.

Now as she reviewed her own individual life she could not but think of the way in which she had been brought into contact with John Giles and wondered if God's Hand was in this, for her. She could not but be conscious that John loved her, John, so retiring, so humble minded, possessing only a poor opinion of himself, having always been derided by his irascible mother; he looked at Marie as a human being might admire a star, lovely, alluring, but beyond that human being's grasp.

His love and admiration was not only known to Marie, but to Gaston and Rachelle as well, but whether John would ever feel that he dare make an offer of marriage to Marie seemed doubtful. His own self-abasement was one hindrance. His mother's rule at home was another, both great barriers in the way of John's bliss.

Marie would never have admitted to another soul that she thought John Giles loved her, she would have considered that an unwomanly thing to do, but her cheek grew rosy as she sat alone at her knitting and thought of him.

" Dear John," she said to herself, " his life is so desolate. He needs someone to care for him and help him to realise his own good qualities. And those poor children how my heart aches for them."

She recalled how only a week or two previously, she had been at the farm and old Mrs. Giles had scolded and nagged at Lawrence and Lovedy, until Lovedy was in tears and Lawrence sullen and scowling. Marie sighed.

" If ever things came to a head, could she share a home with such a tyrant as old Mrs. Giles ? " So her thoughts ran. A firm look came on Marie's face. Although so gentle a character, yet Marie could be resolute, should occasion arise for such conduct. If ever she became John's wife, she was determined that he and the children should be no longer bullied. Marie, with her motherly instincts, was capable of rising in defence of any one who was being ill treated.

At the farm Mrs. Giles was conscious of her son's liking for Marie Durand, nothing escaped her shrewd, old eyes. She took a delight in picturing to the children what terrors life would hold for them if ever they had a stepmother. Neither Lawrence or Lovedy ever thought of Marie Durand as likely to fill this position. She was André and Ninon's aunt and to them a fixture in the Durand household.

One evening John Giles came in to Canterbury and having a little time to spare went to see M. Durand. Gaston was alone, Rachelle, Marie and the young folk were at a neighbour's house for a festive gathering. Gaston welcomed his friend and presently John began to talk about his home life and of the most recent cause for his unhappiness.

"I am troubled about my boy," he said. "You know he is fourteen now and a big lad for his age, but my mother treats him as if he were a two-year-old, in some ways. She was displeased with him lately for some trivial fault, and to punish him said he must sit by himself at meals and have nothing but rye bread. This has been going on for three days and it has nearly broken my heart to sit down to good food and see my boy starving on such miserable diet."

"I should think so indeed. You say your mother treats him like a two-year-old, but I should think no one would be so brutal to a baby."

"Well no, but I mean she orders him about so. This morning the lad lost his temper, got up from his seat and came to our table saying: 'I'm not going to put up with this any longer. I'm going to have some proper food.' His grandmother rushed at him and hit him with a rod, she was in a furious temper at his defying her and before I could interfere, I fear I am slow, the boy turned on her, wrenched the stick from her hand and struck her across her shoulders. Of course I could not allow that, I was obliged to thrash him and send him to his room. As he went he muttered: 'I shall run away, nobody loves me here.' Poor little Lovedy has ben crying most of the day and I feel wretched."

John stopped and Gaston said gravely: "Giles, you must be firm, you cannot have your children's lives ruined, you must act on their behalf. Why don't you marry again? And then tell your mother she must give up both the housekeeping and the control of the children."

"Marry! Ah Durand would that I could! But could I ask the one I love to share such a home as mine? How happy I should be if she would, but I dare not ask."

"I think you might if you are prepared to back up your wife in every way. You speak as though you have someone in your mind," Gaston said with a merry twinkle in his eye.

John Giles had no idea how transparent he had been in his silent admiration of Marie Durand, he thought Durand was quite ignorant of his desire. He hesitated. Then he said in a tense voice: "Durand. I—I perhaps you will be offended if I tell you what I have in my mind."

"Not I, you can trust me."

"Well, I should count myself happy, the most fortunate of men if I could—could win your sister, but she is so far above me in every way. I dare not try."

"Tut, tut, man! I cannot say I really know my sister's sentiments, but I should advise your trying. Don't be fainthearted and don't be too humble. You don't think enough of yourself."

Giles laughed. M. Durand was glad to hear that laugh. A laugh often betrays character and John's laugh was so frank, so boylike and good natured, that Gaston felt, as he had in a measure before, that here was a man to whom he could trust his sister.

"A man who lived with my mother would need to be conceited indeed if he could manage to think anything of himself," John said, then he added: "I called to-day to ask if you would all come out to the farm one day next week. If this beautiful weather continues we shall be making hay, and the young folk will enjoy playing in the hay field and having their tea there. Do come, it will give Lawrence much pleasure."

Gaston accepted the invitation and when his family came in they all hoped the fine weather would last.

When the day which John Giles had fixed, came round it was hot and sunny. At breakfast that morning Gaston said: "I will go round to the Inn and hire two horses for this afternoon. André and I can walk, but you Rachelle and Marie would only arrive hot and tired, and not able to enjoy the picnic."

"Thank you dear. That will be pleasant," Rachelle said, while Leonie asked: "Shall I ride, please let me ride."

"Yes puppet, you will ride with Aunt Marie and Ninon with mother," Gaston told the child.

"And what shall I wear?" was Leonie's next question.

"I know," she continued before Rachelle could reply, "I'll wear my pink silk taffeta, my long silk mittens and my necklace."

"No dear, you cannot go to a hay field dressed like that. You and Ninon will wear your gingham frocks and white bonnets, then you can play as you like and there will be nothing to spoil," was the answer Leonie got.

Leonie pouted, while Ninon said: "You are vain Leonie, always thinking about clothes."

Tears came into Leonie's eyes and André said quickly: "You will look very pretty Leonie in your blue frock and white bonnet, so don't fret, darling."

Leonie's smile returned at André's words. She was never cross for many minutes, sunshine quickly followed storm with her.

Madame Durand's face was grave. André, now a tall lad of sixteen, for they had been in England two years, was looking at Leonie with such an expression of tender admiration on his face that the mother felt troubled, she she could not but see that André's devotion for Leonie was not abating. In his sight she could neither do nor say anything amiss. Leonie, in her childish way, adored him, but her disposition seemed shallow. She was attractive, daily growing prettier, and many people petted her, gave her presents and little treats, all of which she accepted prettily and graciously, as a matter of course for which she did not feel nor show any great gratitude. Ninon was so often passed over, that when any one showed her attention, her pleasure was pathetic. But Madame Durand was glad to see that Ninon tried hard to overcome jealousy of Leonie. It was a battle not won in a day and Madame Durand was very touched one evening when she heard Ninon praying by her bed saying earnestly: " Oh Lord Jesus be in my heart and turn out the evil jealousy. Help me to be glad when Leonie gets all the best."

Ninon's prayer was being answered and she bade fair to be a girl of sterling worth.

Madame Durand looking at her family that morning said to herself:

" I will not worry. André is but a boy still and Leonie only a child. I will try not to look forward to the future, but live a day at a time and trust to God to plan for my children. I suppose all mothers are a bit anxious as to what type of girls their sons will choose for wives."

Chapter XXIII

THE ACCIDENT

THAT afternoon in the hay field Rachelle Durand was quick to note things were happening as they usually did. Leonie was riding triumphantly round the field. André was leading the horse and John Giles walked by the side, with a hand on Leonie to ensure her safety. Rachelle looked round for Ninon and was pleased to see she was deep in conversation with Lawrence. The boy looked brighter than usual, the two children seemed happy together. Lovedy was alone, looking rather disconsolate, so Rachelle joined her and succeeded in bringing a smile to her little, wistful face.

Presently when Leonie's ride ended they all had a game in the hay, then followed tea. Immediately after that, John said the men were coming to put the hay into cocks, as he thought the weather looked like breaking. Everybody was willing to help, each eager to make as many cocks as possible.

It was not long before Marie discovered that Leonie was missing and she said to her sister-in-law: "Leonie has wandered. I do not expect she has gone far. I'll go and look for her."

"Thank you dear," Rachelle said. "I expect she has gone into the next field, I saw her near the gateway not many minutes ago."

So Marie went into the next field, but Leonie was not in sight. Marie hesitated which way to go, then decided to get to the farmyard, for she remembered that at tea time John had told Leonie about some tiny chickens and it seemed probable that Leonie had gone to see them.

At any rate she found that Leonie had gone to the farmyard, for when she got there she caught sight of a blue frock inside a barn. Marie entered just as Leonie had lifted the lid of a big box, and found what she called, " a dear, little, bunny rabbit."

Alas for Leonie; it was no innocent rabbit but a ferret she had found and the animal fastened its teeth on the child's finger. Leonie screamed with pain and terror and Marie rushed forward to her rescue. The ferret loosened its hold on Leonie but sprang savagely at Marie and bit her arm. She was able to beat it off and seizing Leonie, hurried out of the barn pulling the door behind her, but with the pain and fright Marie fainted and sank on the ground unconscious.

Now it happened that five minutes before John Giles had broken his rake and by a quicker route than Marie had taken, gone back to the farm to get another. He heard screams as he drew near and ran forward to find Marie still and white on the ground, and Leonie screaming loudly.

John knelt beside Marie, lifting her head on his arm, exclaiming: " Marie, my love, my dearest; what has happened. Speak to me, my darling."

It was only a brief faint and Marie became dimly aware that someone was calling her by many endearing titles. The voice seemed to come from a long distance, but she struggled to open her eyes and sit up. The colour came back into her face as she realised who it was that was speaking to her.

" O—h, I'm better ! " she said and her voice was only a gasp, but it grew steadier after a moment and she tried to explain what had happened.

Meanwhile Leonie was crying piteously. Her finger was bleeding badly and the sight of blood combined with the fright of seeing Marie lying unconscious had naturally upset the child. John took her in his arms and asking Marie to take his arm and lean on him he took them into the house.

Prudence, the old servant who had cared for John in his babyhood came to see what was the matter and quickly took in the situation.

" La, la, to be sure ! That beast of a ferret. But there the little missie had no right to be opening the box. Come in m'm. I'll soon bind up the wounds."

Talking all the time Prudence soon brought linen bandages and set to work. John dispatched a farm hand to the field to bring Madame Durand and then asked Prudence: " Where is the mistress ? "

" Upstairs in her own room Master. Shall I send Sarah to call her ? "

" No, I will go and explain to her what has happened. But give Mademoiselle Durand one of your reviving cordials Prudence, as soon as you have finished bandaging. Are you sure Marie you are feeling better. Can I do anything to help you ? "

He hovered over her as she lay back in the roomy, armchair Prudence had placed for her. Marie noticed he had called her by her Christian name, a thing he had never done before."

Leonie was feeling that she was getting insufficient attention and said peevishly: " I'm hurt too."

" I'm going to see to you in a minute," Prudence said. " You were a naughty girl, you know."

" I'm not naughty." Leonie's cries began to be more violent until John said gravely: " Leonie, stop crying at once you are worrying your aunt."

Marie sat up. " Oh don't scold her. I am still a bit dazed or I should have attended to her first or rather asked you to do so, Prudence."

" I will now," Prudence said grimly.

Mistress Giles had not joined the picnic party in the hay field, but considering that she was over seventy years of age, this was excusable. Now at her son's request she came into the hall. She was a trifle glum, but being a gentlewoman by birth and education she could not but be courteous to an injured guest, in rather a distant fashion. She inquired how the accident had happened and then much to Leonie's annoyance said: "I hope Mademoiselle Durand you will not fail to give this naughty child a severe chastisement for such shocking behaviour. Leaving the field without permission, evincing such curiosity as to open a chest which did not belong to her parents, although had it done so, to raise the lid without permission merited punishment, her behaviour is terrible."

Leonie whose loud cries had ceased, and was now lying on a settle looking rather pale broke into tears again, saying: "Go away you horrid, old woman."

"Leonie, Leonie you must not speak like that." Marie said, while John added: "Oh come mother, surely the child has had sufficient punishment. Her finger was severely nipped, and the fright too will have taught her a lesson."

Mistress Giles looked her annoyance, but she refrained from arguing the matter. She turned to Marie with a stiff: "Is there anything more we can do for you, Mademoiselle ?"

"I am indeed sorry to have given all this trouble" Marie said.

At this moment Rachelle and Gaston arrived, both looking anxious, having scarcely understood from the farm boy's report what had happened. They were relieved to find things were no worse. Rachelle Durand sat down and took Leonie on her lap and soon soothed her ruffled feelings. Mistress Giles' lips curled with contempt at the sight of the child being petted instead of punished.

Then a discussion took place as to how best to get to

Canterbury. Marie declared she was well enough to ride, but John had another plan, he insisted on sending a farm hand on horseback to the town and from "Ye Chequers Inn," hiring a coach. No argument shook him in his determination, so the others gave way, discovering for the first time that John could insist on doing what he thought right. Gaston's respect for him grew.

Meanwhile Mistress Giles ordered refreshment to be brought. She told Marie that a drink of "Lamb's wool" was what she needed. Marie found the drink rather disagreeable and could not understand how English people liked it so much. It was a mixture of ale and apple pulp made hot and sweetened with honey. Marie managed to get it down rather than offend the old lady, while Gaston and Rachelle begged to be excused from partaking of anything as they had so recently had a hearty meal in the hayfield.

While they waited for the coach to arrive, John was longing to get Marie alone, but did not see how he was to accomplish it. Presently however Gaston went back to the hayfield to fetch the others and Madame Durand asked if she might wash Leonie's face as she had rubbed her soiled hands over her cheeks, and her tears had added to the dirty appearance. Mistress Giles took them to another room for the ablution. So for a short time John and Marie were alone.

John drew a chair close to her and made a rush at what he wanted to say.

"Marie, if I may call you Marie, did you hear what I said when you were just coming around from that swoon?"

"I did, John," Marie answered simply.

"Ah, then you know how I feel towards you. Can you, do you? I mean do you think I could teach you to love me? I'm only a blundering country man and I feel it is like asking a beautiful, singing bird to wed a dingy bat, but"—John was surprised at his own burst of eloquence. A sound of footsteps coming, hastened him. "Marie, Marie, just say one word. Say 'Yes.'"

Marie smiled, and with shining eyes said: "Yes John."

That was enough, John's diffident air seemed to have dropped from him. He stood erect with a new look of manly determination about him. Gaston coming in at that moment said to himself: "Things are happily settled I can see."

Chapter XXIV

A GLAD SURPRISE

THAT evening when Madame Durand was brushing Ninon's hair before going to bed, Ninon said suddenly: "What is a stepmother?"

Madame Durand explained to the child and then said: "Why do you ask, Ninon?"

"Mother, Lawrence says his grandmother tells him he is going to have a stepmother soon and she will be very hard and cruel, he will get lots more punishment then than he does now. Are all stepmothers cruel, mother?"

"No indeed. Lawrence's grandmother is quite wrong. I am sure that when Lawrence has a stepmother she will be kind to him and to Lovedy. They will be quite happy."

"Oh I'm so glad. I wish I had known that, but I will tell him when I see him again. Perhaps that won't be for ever so long."

"I daresay you and André could walk out to the farm one day soon and then you could tell him."

"That would be nice. I don't want poor Lawrence to be unhappy. Mother if I tell you a secret, you won't tell anyone will you?"

"I never tell your secrets, darling."

"No I know you don't. Lawrence said he had made up his mind as soon as the stepmother comes to run away. But I told him what the pastor said on Sunday."

"What was that, dear?"

"It was about David. How he faced the giant and he said: 'Boys and girls remember, cowards run away from their difficulties and often find they have harder things to face than the difficulties they fled from.' I told Lawrence that, and he says he will try to be brave and face his difficulties, for one reason he thinks it would not do to take Lovedy with him and yet it would be cruel to leave her. I thought perhaps she could come and live with us, but I didn't say so, for that would have made it easier for him to run away."

The hair brushing had finished now and Ninon put on her bedgown and knelt for her evening prayer.

When she rose from her knees she whispered to her mother: " Mother I asked Lawrence if he thought Leonie very pretty and he said, ' She is all right, but I like your face much the best.' Mother, I do like Lawrence very much, and we've promised to be always friends."

Madame Durand kissed her little daughter and said: " I'm so glad you were sensible and gave Lawrence good advice. He is a nice friend for you to have, dear."

" Dear child," she said to herself as she went downstairs, " God help me to always keep her confidence."

There seemed no reason for a long courtship for John and Marie. John was eager to bring his bride home. He spoke plainly to his mother and told her that Marie would take over the housekeeping and the entire management of the children. He said tactfully: " Things have been too much for you lately, Mother. Now you can rest and take life quietly."

Mistress Giles had the sense to see when she was beaten. It was true that she had been feeling worn for some time which had made her more difficult than ever. So now she said coldly: " You are master here John and I have no choice but to submit. When you bring your wife here I shall keep to my own room and Prudence can wait on me. It will not be long before the old mother is under the ground and all she has done for you will be forgotten."

"Come, come Mother, you must not talk like that," John said.

Mistress Giles hastened to leave the room so her son had not the opportunity of saying more, or of noticing that her thin, old lips trembled and her eyes dimmed with tears. She had been her own enemy, an overbearing desire for her own way had spoiled her life and now her old age could not but be an unhappy one.

John felt strangely shy at the thought of having to tell his boy and girl of his intentions and pondered long as to how best he could break the news. He almost thought of leaving the matter until he brought his bride home and then give them a glad surprise, but he feared that they might hear of his engagement from the Durand children and he did not wish them to get information in that fashion.

He was still wondering how and when he should tell the children, when one day entering a barn he heard voices coming from the loft overhead. This particular spot was much beloved by Lawrence and Lovedy as almost the only place where they could get away from their grandmother, for she would not attempt to climb the ricketty ladder that reached their hiding spot. Here, they retired to talk over their grievances, here, they kept sundry treasures that their grandmother would have condemned as rubbish, among them an old wooden doll dear to Lovedy, and a box containing a collection of birds' eggs which interested Lawrence. There was plenty of soft, sweet-smelling hay scattered on the floor which made comfortable seats and often the two had long happy hours there together.

As John entered the barn he heard Lovedy say: "Grandmother says the stepmother is coming soon now. Lawrence you won't run away, and leave me will you?"

"No, I've made up my mind to put up with it. Ninon

says only cowards run away from their difficulties. I promised her I wouldn't."

"Why does father bring home a stepmother? Is he obliged to do it?"

"No, of course not. I s'pose he thinks it will make him happy . . . ."

"Well then we must try not to mind too much, even if she is cruel, I should like poor father to be happy." Lovedy said.

John started. He felt very touched at his little daughter's desire for his happiness. And he had had no idea of his children's dread. It opened his eyes to much.

He called up to them "I'm coming up dears. I want to have a talk."

Lawrence and Lovedy looked at each other in surprise and wondered if their conversation had been overheard.

"I have something important to tell you both, something that I hope will make you very happy," John said, as he sat down on a heap of hay and pulled Lovedy towards him, putting his arm around her.

He felt he must delay no longer so said without preamble: "I'm going to give you a dear, dear mother."

"Do you mean a stepmother? Lovedy inquired.

"We will not call her that, dear. I want you to say 'mother.' Now can you guess who it is?"

Both the children said "no."

"Why I thought you would easily guess. I must tell you, it is dear Mademoiselle Marie Durand. I am sure you will both love her, she loves you and wants you to be happier than you have ever been. So you will give her a warm welcome, won't you?"

Lawrence jumped to his feet quite stirred out of his usual apathy: "Why father she is lovely." While Lovedy said: "I thought she belonged to the Durands."

"She is going to belong to us now, Lovedy. So we are all pleased."

"Oh yes, yes," both the children said heartily.

"But what will grandmother say?" Lawrence asked.

"Grandmother is going to leave everything to mother now."

John kissed Lovedy and put an affectionate arm round his son. He heaved a sigh of relief that the telling was over.

So happier days dawned for the household at the farm. Marie's sweet gracious rule brought joy to all. John was amazed to see how his children blossomed out like flowers in the sunshine and even old Mistress Giles, although she kept to her determination to spend her closing days in her own apartment, seemed to grow more gentle under her daughter-in-law's influence.

Chapter XXV

PIERRE BENOIT

THE pitiless sun with its scorching rays beat down on the bare heads and backs of the galley slaves as they bent with strained muscles at the oars. Splash, splash, with monotonous rhythm came the dipping of the blades, the only other sounds being the harsh word of command, the swish of the lash as it fell on some unfortunate rower, or muttered oaths and curses. The countenances of most of the men were indicative of their characters, rough, coarse, repellent, there was, however, one exception, a man young in years, yet with a face that spoke of deep suffering, in spite of which a look of peace shone in his eyes, and brave, quiet courage lent a firm line to his lips.

The young man was Pierre Benoit, who for three long years had worked as a galley slave, each successive year seeming harder than the last.

True at first the suffering both mental and physical was terrible to endure, the separation from his loved Jacqueline, the hopelessness of his position, the heavy labour, the constant sting of the lash as it fell from the hand of the overseer on his bare back, the scanty food, all seemed more than the human frame could long sustain. Pierre at times took consolation from the thought that life could not last under such conditions, and yet again he felt it hard that his life should be cut off in its youth. However there were certain things that helped to alleviate in a slight measure the anguish. For one thing he was with his own countrymen and co-religionists. Jacques Goyer sat in the bench next to him, an old pastor from another province was near by, they were all

Huguenots and at night in the hold of the ship, or snatching what sleep they could on the benches, they consoled one another with hymns, prayers, passages of Scripture and exhortations. In the darkness of the night, songs arose and a sense of the Presence of the Saviour filled their hearts with a joy only known to those who suffer for His sake. This fellowship meant a tremendous lot to them all. But as the months passed, things changed. Several died. To Pierre's intense grief, Jacques Goyer was one of the first. The old pastor, who had strengthened them all with his messages, followed Jacques. Then a few were shifted to other boats, until at last Pierre was left alone with a crew of wicked men, who had been sent to the galleys, as a well merited punishment, for horrible crimes.

It was now more than ever that Pierre suffered. Instead of hymns and Scriptures at night he heard oaths and curses. The men fought sometimes with one another. Pierre felt he had reached the depths of agony that any human being could endure and he wondered that he went on living. Sometimes he became so dazed that he laboured at the oar as though he were a mere machine unable to stop, but at other times, he was uplifted as he whispered to himself words of prayer, or said over and over again verses of Scripture learnt in the old bygone happy days. Then it was that he felt Christ standing by him, then it was that a Voice sounded in his heart: " Lo I am with you all the days."

Pierre's worn face, furrowed, as it was already, with lines of suffering, yet shone with a light not human but divine.

At regular intervals the men were visited by various priests who came to hear confessions and administer the mass. Pierre was a puzzle to most of these visitors, for he quietly but firmly refused their offices, some left him alone in despair, others in cruel hate saw that he suffered at the hands of the overseer, in consequence of his refusal.

Then at the end of three years a new priest was appointed to the task of ministering to these poor galley slaves. One Abbé Jean Bion. He was quick to see the difference in Pierre and the other men. He knew the reason Pierre was there, for before taking over his duties he had studied the crime list and knew the accusation of each man. Abbé Jean Bion was sincere in his work and honestly desired to help them all to a better state of mind. He started with high hopes of reforming the slaves and if possible bettering their condition.

Pierre attracted him immensely, and he said to himself: "Now if I can convert this man to the true faith I might be able to secure his release. This should not prove a difficult task."

* The Abbé visited the men frequently, watching them closely. His tender heart bled at the sight of their suffering, although he felt that most of them deserved punishment. But to know that on many of the boats were men, only there because of their religion, brought tears to his eyes.

He tried his best to influence the rough men by teaching them prayers to the saints, by inducing them to confess to him, but he felt his labours were in vain, and as to his protests to the overseer, when he tried to persuade him to be less ready with the lash, he found that the man, although seemingly polite, only jeered at him behind his back and by no means softened the barbarity of his treatment.

On the morning in question, when the heat was almost intolerable, the Abbé came on board the boat and sitting by Pierre as he had done many times before, tried once

* Historical person. He wrote about that time in his diary; "Their blood preached to me and I felt myself a Protestant." See SMILES' *Huguenots*.

again to get him to renounce his religion and signify his willingness to go to mass.

"Listen, Benoit," the Abbé said, "I believe I can secure your release if you will but yield. Do not be obstinate. I seek your good. I want to help you and you could return to your home, find the girl you love and be happy."

Pierre had one day told the Abbé about Jacqueline, for the kindly man invited confidence.

For a few minutes Pierre was silent. A wave of temptation swept over him, it was the tempter's hour of opportunity. A vision of freedom, the chance of seeking for Jacqueline, of being once more a man and not a machine, of mixing with congenial companions, of escaping the lash, the oaths, the heat and the coarse food. Nothing was omitted in that vision as pressed home by the tempter of souls.

Abbé Jean Bion saw the wistful expression on the man's face and waited. But even as he did, a new look came into Pierre's eyes, for the vision changed, Pierre became conscious of One standing beside him, Whose Hands outstretched to him were pierced. Pierre heard a Voice that said: "I suffered for thee, canst thou not bear for Me?"

Pierre was strengthened and turning his face towards the Abbé he said simply: "I cannot deny my Lord."

Even as he spoke his head dropped forward on his breast and the Abbé saw that Pierre was unconscious. Now the Abbé in virtue of his position had a certain amount of authority and he asserted it. The overseer gave in when the Abbé insisted that the boat must be rowed into Toulon and that he, the Abbé, must be allowed to take charge of Benoit.

So it came to pass that when Benoit opened his eyes, he found himself lying on a couch, covered with a cool, linen sheet and standing by him a motherly looking woman who was watching him with great concern.

"Where am I?" Pierre gasped in astonishment.

"Ah, now you are coming round, my man" the woman said. "The Abbé had you brought here an hour ago. He wants me to nurse you for a bit, so lie still and do not talk."

The woman bustled away and presently returned with a basin of broth. Raising Pierre's head she fed him with a spoon of the savoury liquid. Pierre thought he had never tasted anything so delicious, in his half-starved, overworked condition it was indeed a treat.

"Now go to sleep," the woman said. "'Tis kitchen physic and rest you need. You'll soon be all right."

Pierre too weary to talk willingly obeyed and fell into a sound slumber that lasted some hours. When he awoke the Abbé was standing in the room looking at him.

Pierre with a shining face said: "Sir, how am I to thank you for all your kindness to me? May the Lord reward you."

The Abbé sat down by the bed. "You are feeling better, Benoit?"

"Yes indeed, thank you sir. I have had a lovely sleep."

The Abbé sat in thought a moment and then he said: "I have told you before Benoit that you are a puzzle to me, in fact all you Huguenots are, and yet, I begin to wonder whether you have not got the true religion. I am obliged to admit that you have a secret source of strength, something that sustains you in affliction. There is something about you that fills my heart with yearning. I started my work as a priest with zeal, with a real honest longing to help people but I have failed. Benoit teach me your secret. Show me how I may possess the something that you have."

The Abbé stretched out his hands with a gesture of

appeal that went to Pierre's heart. He raised himself on his arm and said: " Sir, it is not a something that you need but a Someone. It is Jesus, the Saviour Who sustains us in our trials. The Lord Jesus, God's Son Who died on the Cross to make an atonement for our sins, Who rose again and lives to-day to succour us. We draw from Him the grace we need, the grace that enables us to endure. He bids us come to Him and take His gift of salvation."

Pierre sank back on his pillow, his earnestness had exhausted him and the Abbé said: " I ought not to let you talk so much. Here comes good Marthe with a meal for you."

" I heard your voices, sir," Marthe said, " so I knew my patient was awake."

The Abbé would not let Pierre talk any longer, but just before the Abbé left the room Pierre said earnestly: " Sir the Saviour says to you ' Come unto me, and I will give you rest.' "

The Abbé left and all that evening and again in the morning, the words sounded with a note of constant pleading, sounded with a strange persistency: " Come unto Me, Come unto Me. Not to the Virgin not a saint, but to Me the One Who died for you, Come unto Me."

The Abbé went about his duties. He visited the sick, he conducted a service, he walked the streets, he sat in his study, he took his meals, but over and over again, with an emphatic insistence, that could not be ignored, came the message: " Come unto Me."

The time came for the Abbé to retire to rest, he knelt before a beautifully carved figure of the Virgin Mary but no words came from his lips for louder and clearer than ever echoed the words: " Come unto Me, and I will give you rest."

It was impossible to sleep. The Abbé was facing all that obedience to that invitation would mean. His position, his work, his friends, his native land all must be left. It was going to cost, the struggle was great. At last he rose from his couch and knelt. The Voice of the Crucified had conquered. With a cry for mercy, with emotion too deep for words at first, the Abbé obeyed the call and came for forgiveness to the Saviour. As he knelt there, a new vision came to him of his own sinfulness and unworthiness, looked up to by his compeers as a saintly man, reverenced by those to whom he had ministered, yet for long, by the power of the Holy Spirit, he had been conscious of the sinfulness of his own heart, now that conviction deepened and he could only plead for forgiveness, for cleansing, and even as he prayed, some words Pierre had used in conversation weeks before came to his mind. "Come now and let us reason together, saith the Lord, though your sins be as scarlet, they shall be as white as snow."

The words brought peace to his troubled mind and his heart was at rest.

Chapter XXVI

THE HOME CALL

NEXT morning when the Abbé awoke, his first thought was one of thanksgiving for the experience of the evening before. Christ was now a Reality to him, a Living Person and One to Whom the Abbé owed allegiance. It was a glad thought yet fraught with tremendous gravity as he pondered on what the future would mean for him. One thing he had already made up his mind about and that was, that if it were at all possible, he must obtain Pierre's freedom. He knew that occasionally the galley slaves were sold, the price being about one hundred and twenty pounds, varying of course according to the age and strength of the slave. Pierre being in a weakened condition might be sold for less, but be that as it may, the Abbé, being a well-to-do man, was not going to make a difficulty of a few pounds more or less.

So accordingly as soon as the Abbé had breakfasted he sought out the governor and expressed the desire to obtain the services of one Pierre Benoit as a personal attendant. The governor saw no occasion for making any difficulties, there followed a short discussion as to the price, the Abbé deeming it wise not to appear too eager or willing to pay a fancy price, or the governor might suspect some other reason than the desire to obtain a suitable servant. Finally it was settled. Pierre's price being eighty pounds, " a bargain," the governor said.

The Abbé shrugged his shoulders and remarked that the bargain was on the governor's side for if Pierre remained in the service of the government, he would die, for the work and hardships were weakening him considerably. The men parted amiably and the Abbé hastened to Pierre's lodging with the papers in his pocket, which, duly signed, gave Pierre his freedom and the right to travel across France to his native town.

Pierre did not seem as surprised as his benefactor had expected. He was exceedingly grateful and tried to express his thanks.

Presently he said: " Sir, this morning God gave me the assurance in my heart that deliverance was near. May He reward you for your great goodness to me."

" Ah Benoit, I am already rewarded, for God has visited me with His salvation."

Pierre was too overwhelmed for speech, but the Abbé saw by the light in Pierre's eyes what joy the news gave him.

Then they discussed the future. " What would you wish to do ? " the Abbé asked.

" Sir I belong to you. It is for you to direct."

" No Benoit, I bought you to give you your freedom," the Abbé told him.

" Sir I would fain serve you, it is the least that I can do."

" But tell me, do you wish to return to your native town ? I am inclined to think there is no safety in France for either of us, alas ! "

" My one desire, sir, is to find Jacqueline."

" Yes of course. You know where to seek for her ? "

" She was in the convent at Niort when I was taken here."

" Then there we will seek her. I shall travel as the Abbé still, and you as my attendant. I must at once procure suitable clothing for you and as soon as you feel able we will start. The sooner the better for our safety."

Pierre declared he was able to go at once, already he felt stronger and he certainly looked it, so the Abbé decided that the very next morning they would be off.

They travelled without any untoward incident for a few days and at every step they advanced, Pierre grew more eager in his longing to be in the neighbourhood where he hoped to get tidings of Jacqueline. They were riding through a small village, the Abbé in front and Pierre following, when a man evidently, the worse for drink, came out of a cottage shouting angrily and waving his arms about in a senseless fashion. His appearance was so sudden, the noise breaking in on the quietness of the country side so unexpected, that the Abbé's horse, a high spirited animal, took fright and bolted.

It tore along at a great rate, Pierre spurring his horse to follow, the man who caused the trouble was shouting more loudly, thus increasing the horse's terror. The road, merely a narrow track, was rough and uneven and to Pierre's horror, he saw the horse stumble and fall as he caught his foot in a hole in the road. The Abbé was flung over the creature's head and lay a crumpled heap in the roadway. It took only a moment for Pierre to reach the Abbé's side. He flung himself off his horse and knelt beside the injured man, whose eyes were closed, and face entirely colourless.

" Sir, sir," Pierre exclaimed in anguish. " Sir, tell me are you much hurt ? "

The Abbé's eyes slowly opened and a half smile swept over his face followed immediately by a contortion of agony.

A man working in a field near by came running and offered advice. " The monastery is only about half a mile away. If we get a door we can carry his reverence there."

Pierre felt somewhat dismayed at the thought of finding help at a monastery, but something must be done at once for the poor sufferer, so he agreed to the suggestion and the farm labourer went off to get the door and another man to help him.

Pierre still knelt by the Abbé's side and raised his head, but the movement only brought a groan from the Abbé, so Pierre placed him gently down again.

"Water, give me water," the Abbé moaned, and the drunken man, now frightened into a measure of sobriety, having reached the scene went to get water.

The Abbé once more opened his eyes. He was quite conscious now and said: "My lad I am finished. I feel this is death."

A long pause, then, "I'm glad, thank God it is all settled."

Again silence. Pierre saw the men approaching, but they were still at a little distance.

Once more the dying man spoke. "Benoit, you will need money to finish your journey. Take my purse, it is inside my coat."

"Don't think of that sir," Pierre said; his heart was wrung at the thought of the loss of his benefactor.

But the Abbé was insistent. "Quick take it. Put it safely away inside your tunic."

So Pierre obeyed and had just bestowed the purse away when the men arrived with the door and together they placed the poor Abbé on it and bore him away to the monastery. The porter, with a glance at the Abbé's clothing, decided that the arrival was of importance and sent a subordinate to call the Prior, who in his turn, sent for a monk who was skilled in surgery and medicine. Brother Nicholas after a brief examination shook his head. He administered a restorative, but in a whisper to his superior expressed his opinion that the injured man could not last long.

Under the influence of the dose Brother Nicholas had given, the Abbé, now resting on a couch in the hall of the monastery, was able to make a few remarks.

Brokenly, with many pauses, he directed Pierre to take a small case from his vest pocket adding to the Prior: " Sir you will find there the address of my only relative, my sister, the Countess de Laval. Please communicate with her."

The effort of speech exhausted the Abbé and Pierre kneeling by his side feared he had spoken his last words.

The Prior, bent on administering the last rites of the church, drew near putting his hand on Pierre's shoulder saying: " Come young man, give me room."

Pierre heeded him not, for at that moment the Abbé spoke again " Tell me Benoit, the words—Though your sins . . . . ."

Pierre repeated the text. " Come now let us reason together, saith the Lord: though your sins be as scarlet, they shall be as white as snow."

The Abbé's eyes opened once more, a smile of exceeding beauty came over his face as he whispered: " White as snow. Put away for ever, forgiven."

The voice sank. A few short, gasping breaths and he was gone.

The Prior spoke angrily: " Unabsolved ! "

Then he turned to Brother Nicholas and conversed in a low tone, Pierre caught the word " heretic."

He felt dazed, it had all happened so swiftly, it seemed impossible to realise that the man who had been so good to him was gone.

The Prior's words broke in on his dulled senses: " I will see you later, young man. I cannot attend to you now." " Here," he beckoned to a monk who stood respectfully in the background, " here take this young man and don't let him out of your sight. I shall need him later."

The monk bade Pierre follow him and conducted him to a small room, a door from which led into a large garden.

Chapter XXVII

PIERRE'S ESCAPE

IN the quiet of that little room, Pierre's thoughts were busy. There was a great sense of loss at the death of his benefactor, for whom he had great affection, an added reason for that being that Pierre had been the instrument in God's Hand to bring the Abbé to Christ. It seemed impossible to grasp the fact that the one who only an hour before had been in health had now passed into the Presence of the Saviour. Pierre felt stunned for a time, but presently he recalled that muttered word from the Prior "heretic." A silent thanksgiving went up from his heart that the dear Abbé was safe, no harm could come to him from any persecutor. But for himself? The outlook was grave. A determination took hold of him, he would get away from the monastery as quickly as possible. But how was that to be done? The monk had received orders to guard him.

Pierre decided to appear at ease, to give no hint that he desired to escape. He hoped by these means the man might be put off his guard. Pierre admired the garden and the monk seemed pleased, for he himself worked there several hours daily. Then Pierre asked when the next meal was due and the monk said he would get some refreshment for Pierre at once. Pierre accepted the offer and was soon partaking of a good meal. While he ate he satisfied the man's curiosity as to how exactly the accident took place. Altogether they chatted as though they were friends of long standing.

Pierre had his eye on the garden and was praying that the opportunity of escape might be given to him.

Presently the door of the room opened and an irate monk stood there.

"You lazy vagabond, I wondered where you were. Leaving me to do your duties, gossiping and wasting your time. Come along at once. The vegetables are not done, nor the dishes washed."

"I have to guard this man, the Prior said so," the monk said in a sulky tone.

"Nonsense, just your laziness. The man can stay here. He can't come to any harm, come along I say."

So Pierre's guardian departed, and Pierre strolled into the garden. He walked leisurely about, now stopping to inhale the scent of a magnificent rose, then standing to watch some bees laden with honey returning to a row of hives which stood against a wall. Pierre appeared to be merely looking round, as long as he was within sight of the monastery windows, but presently he turned into a path which led to a thick hedge. The moment the hedge sheltered him from view, his movements altered, he sped along the path hurriedly. The garden was spacious, but everywhere was bounded by high walls. He turned into the kitchen garden, there, a row of fruit trees grew against the wall. Here was Pierre's chance. He could see a figure in the distance at work, but the man's back was towards him and he was stooping over some small plants.

It was now or never. With a silent cry for help, Pierre climbed a sturdy espalier, its branches did not reach the top of the wall by some feet, but Pierre was desperate, he could reach the edge of the wall with his fingers and with a mighty effort, made possible by the iron muscles of his arms, developed by his work at the oars, pulled himself up, swung over and dropped on the grassy sward on the other side. For a moment he stood still, then lifting his hat, he said fervently "Thank God."

He found he was now in a field and he hurried across

to a gate on the opposite side, which opened into a narrow track. His great object was to get as far away as possible from the monastery and he walked rapidly. He thought longingly of the good horse he had left behind at the monastery, but to return was impossible so he trudged on. It was a lovely summer evening, gradually the light faded, but Pierre dared not rest. On, on, through the hours of the night he travelled. Once he heard the gallop of horses' feet behind him and he hid in the shelter of a hedge, wondering whether the Prior had sent someone in pursuit of him. Soon after that, he reached the high road and as the light of day dawned and the birds began the song of a new day, to his joy, he recognised the road, he was about five miles from his native town.

He felt worn and was in need of food but he pressed on. Thinking things over as he went, he decided to call at the house of a neighbour of former days. He and his wife were Roman Catholics, but friendly folk, and Pierre felt that, for the sake of old times, they would aid him.

He reached the little, two-roomed house, just as the man and his wife were having breakfast, ere the man started for his day's work.

At first neither recognised Pierre, and little wonder, for he had changed from a smooth-faced lad to a bearded man and looked much older than his twenty-two years. However as soon as they knew it was Pierre Benoit they welcomed him warmly, exclaiming in amazement that he was still alive. They plied him with questions, but before replying he asked one thing: "Tell me, what happened to my mother?"

"Ah Pierre, she died the day you were taken. The shock finished her, and it was a mercy, for she would have fretted sorely for you."

Pierre was not surprised. His mother had been having heart attacks for some time before his arrest. He had always thought she must have passed away.

"Now," said the good housewife, drawing up a chair to the table, "come and have some breakfast. You look as though you needed it."

"I do," Pierre agreed.

Pierre told them he had been walking all night and would be glad of a rest. The man had to leave for his days' toil, he said as he was leaving: "You get a good sleep to-day Pierre, and I'll hear your story to-night."

Turning to his wife he said: "Better not say anything to the neighbours, Gabrielle. We don't want trouble," and Gabrielle agreed.

How good it was presently to stretch his weary limbs on a low bed. Pierre gave a sigh of contentment. He was too tired at the moment to consider his future steps. Sleep he must, and in a very few minutes slumber had come, and through the long hours of that day, held him fast.

In the evening he told his story. His listeners ejaculated with many expressions of astonishment, and in their turn told Pierre many items of news. They complained that the neighbourhood was much the worse for the departure of the Protestants.

"Why," Gabrielle said, "I dare not go out after dark for the streets are not safe, lawless ruffians roam about. Give me the psalm singing Huguenots, although they may be mistaken in their religious views, rather than those who are left."

Her husband took up the story. "You see Pierre, men scoff at what the priests tell them. They see it is a money making affair. So much to pay before a mass can be said for the soul of your friend, pay for this, pay for that. I, for one don't wonder that people are turning from religion. Our country will soon be without any at all."

Pierre spoke of the true religion, of Christ the Saviour. The two listened gravely, but made no comment. Then

Pierre went on to say: " I must now get to the convent at Niort and see if I can get any information about Jacqueline." He had told them about the day of his arrest and how he had discovered that Jacqueline was in the convent.

The man's face was troubled. Once shut up in a convent the Huguenots seldom escaped. It seemed hopeless for Pierre to make any inquiry, he would be only running into danger for himself, but to the advice given, Pierre turned a deaf ear. Go he must. So then his friend suggested a disguise. The Prior of the monastery from which Pierre had escaped had a reputation for hunting down heretics. He would be annoyed at Pierre having slipped through his hands, he might have spies anywhere. Beside which the monastery and the convent had some connection, so the man had heard, although just what that connection was he did not know, except that he thought the Prior went there sometimes to receive the confession of the mother superior.

Then they discussed what the disguise should be. Gabrielle had a sudden inspiration.

" Why Pierre, you used to be good at playing the cornemuse * (French bagpipes). Now if you shave your beard, wear the dress of a travelling musician, you will not be recognised. I can stain your face with walnut juice to give you a foreign look."

" A splendid idea. But where can I get the clothes ? "

" I can get them at the old clothes shop if you have any money Pierre, to pay for them " Gabrielle's husband said.

Pierre was thankful to recall the Abbé's thoughtfulness in providing him with funds. He shuddered as he remembered the gift, for had he been detained in the

---

* Bagpipes were originally French. They were introduced into Scotland by Mary Queen of Scots. The harp being the national musical instrument of Scotland.

monastery he would probably have been searched and accused of stealing the Abbé's purse. He had indeed had a narrow escape.

So it was decided that Pierre was to have another quiet day. On the morrow the good man would bring the necessary clothes when he returned from his work. Gabrielle seemed pleased at the way her suggestion had been taken up, and when next evening she saw him dressed and equipped with his cornemuse, she exclaimed with delight for he certainly looked quite a different man than on the day of his arrival. Then he appeared to be a gentleman's well-groomed servant, now he was a shabbily, but gaudily attired, musician. He wore a black velvet coat with somewhat soiled lace at neck and sleeves, a false black moustache gave the finishing touch to his now dark face, in place of the fair beard. Pierre felt that even if he met the Prior himself he could not be recognised.

Chapter XXVIII

A FRIENDLY GOSSIP

NEXT morning Pierre was off.

"Good luck to you," said his hostess, as he left, after having pressed on her acceptance a golden louis d'or, as payment for what he had received.

"Poor fellow," she added turning to her husband as she watched Pierre's departing figure. "He will never find his girl, he is doomed to disappointment."

"I am afraid that is so. They never get out of convents, once they get in," her husband replied.

Pierre would have felt as hopeless as they did, had it not been for his faith in God. Now as he walked on, he prayed for guidance and trusted that God, Who had accomplished his deliverance, would still be his Guide.

He reached the vicinity of the convent the following day and walked round its outer wall. But what to do next he knew not or how to set about making inquiries. He felt as helpless as a little child and could only continue to look to the God of all wisdom for direction. He determined to try to make friends with someone connected with the convent, the porter perhaps, but although he played his best at the entrance gate, the surly porter was not attracted.

Pierre retired to a cottage and got a lodging for the night and again next day he started out on his errand. As he drew near the convent he noticed a buxom lass, carrying a basket of eggs, enter the yard and he thought to himself: "When she comes out I will try and get a word with her.

He waited at a little distance and presently she

appeared swinging her empty basket and singing a little song.

Pierre started playing and placed himself in her pathway. The girl stopped to listen and Pierre, after a moment or two, ceased playing, lifted his hat with a polite gesture and wished her "Good-day," paying her a compliment by saying: "You have a charming voice, Mademoiselle, I heard your song as you came along."

The girl laughed heartily. She was a plump, good-natured looking soul and did not seem at all disinclined for conversation.

"May I carry your basket for you Mademoiselle, and walk a while with you? Pierre asked.

The girl again laughed.

"La, there's no weight in my basket now it's empty. I haven't far to go either, only across the field to the farm, but you can come along and play to my old grandmother. She's blind poor old soul and she loves a tune."

"That I will with pleasure, Mademoiselle. Do you often go to the convent?"

"Twice a week with eggs and poultry."

"Then you know many of the inmates likely."

"Yes I know some." She rattled off a string of names.

"Did I hear they had some women and girls there who were heretics? Perhaps you know some of them?"

"No I don't know any of them, but I've heard my mother say they are terribly obstinate and difficult. But my mother knows more about the folks there, because she is a great friend of a lay-sister, who is the cook. Mother often goes to see her and hears all the gossip of the place."

"Then perhaps your mother will be able to tell me something about—about, a friend of mine, who I believe is there."

"A friend!" The girl laughed again. She seemed to find many things to amuse her. "A friend, now I'll be bound 'tis your sweetheart you'm asking about. La, la, to be sure !"

"Well have it that way if you like, Mademoiselle," Pierre said falling in with the girl's mood and laughing with her.

By the time they had reached the farm they were chatting as if they were old friends and the farmer's wife looking out the window said to her old blind mother: "Here comes Matilde. Who's she picked up with now ? Bless the girl, she collects boys like a pot of honey collecting wasps. 'Tis a musician I see. He's got a cornemuse, so you'll have a tune, mother."

Pierre obliged by playing for a time to the old lady, then seeing he looked tired the farmer's wife said: "Now you'd better stop and I'll give you something to eat."

Pierre took the opportunity of asking a few questions while eating. The woman was thoughtful.

"H-m-m yes. 'Twas a matter of three years agone or more that those heretic women and girls were brought here. I wonder which of them you want to know about."

"A young girl with lovely golden hair, long thick plaits," Pierre explained.

"Why yes. That would be the one the Abbess was so annoyed about. My friend Sister Agathe told me the story. One of the young lady boarders, Mademoiselle Catherine de Vere, took a fancy to this girl and when her schooling was finished she asked the Abbess to let her have the girl as her maid. The Abbess consented, on one condition, that if Mademoiselle de Vere had not succeeded in making the girl a convert in a year, back to the convent she was to come to be dealt with. And la! 'twas really a joke on the Abbess, when the year was up and the Abbess sent for a report, she finds the shoe on the other foot, so to speak, the girl converted Mademoiselle to her way of thinking and they're both gone off to a foreign land. And not only Mademoiselle and the heretic girl, but Mademoiselle's brother too, a fine young officer in the king's army. I mind him well, for he used to come to see his sister."

Pierre was listening eagerly. The woman went on with her story, pleased to have so interested a listener.

"La! Sister Agathe said 'twould do the old woman good to be thwarted for once. They did laugh about it in the kitchen."

Pierre's relief on hearing that Jacqueline had escaped was too great for words. He only murmured to himself: "Thank God."

Presently he asked: "Which country have they gone to?"

"I don't remember. I'm not sure that I heard, but there, 'twill be sure to be England, I reckon, so many go there, at least so I'm told. I don't know anything about it myself and why people can't be quiet and peaceable and leave religion alone to them who understand it, I can't make out at all."

Pierre tried to explain, saying how each one was responsible and how much it meant to know of one's own salvation. But the woman was not inclined to listen, she said emphatically: "I don't hold with ordinary folk like us meddling in what isn't our business."

She then went out of the kitchen and Pierre was left alone with the old grandmother. She had been listening to what Pierre had been saying and she now said in a whisper: "Did you say one could know one's salvation? I'm old and I'll soon have to die and I'm afraid. I can't sleep for thinking about the pains of purgatory."

Pierre went close to her and said: "Grandmother, Jesus died on the Cross to bear the punishment for your sins."

The old woman interrupted. "Sins, sins, they pile up about me. I remember so many. Tell me how can I get rid of them?"

"Listen, the Blood of Jesus Christ cleanseth from all sin. Not your prayers or penances, not masses said for your soul, but His Blood. Ask Him to make you clean now and He will."

The old woman put her hands together and began: "Oh Mary Mother of God . . . ."

Pierre interrupted, "Oh no grandmother, not that. Come to Jesus for yourself. He says, 'Come unto Me and I will give you rest.'"

"I don't understand. How can I dare, a sinner, to come to the Holy Christ?"

"God's Word tells us it was said when Christ was on earth. 'This Man receiveth sinners.' And, praise His Name, it is true to-day."

A look of determination came into the old woman's face.

"I will come to Him. I've tried coming to the Virgin over and over again and I'm still unforgiven. I'll try Jesus."

The farmer's wife came back then and the grandmother whispered: "Hush."

So Pierre left, thanking God for His leading; news of Jacqueline he had obtained and had had the joy of telling this hungry soul the way of life.

He determined to get to England as soon as possible and continue his hunt for Jacqueline.

Chapter XXIX

THE COMING OF THE PRINCE

ON the evening of November 5th 1688, the folk of the little fishing town of Brixham in Devon were all agog with excitement, mixed with a certain amount of fear, for there on the horizon was to be seen a mighty fleet of vessels, sixty ships of war, and seven hundred transports, slowly, but surely, drawing nearer and nearer the harbour.

"Whoever can they be ?" One man said to another as they stood and watched.

"'Tis I fear they Frenchies," was the reply.

The lord of the manor here appeared and set some fears at rest.

"They are Dutch vessels," he said, "I have heard rumours for some time passed that we might expect them, for our leaders have sent an invitation to William, Prince of Orange, to come to our aid."

"And why sir, do we need his aid ?" queried one.

"To protect the civil and religious liberty of the people. Our foolish King James has alienated the larger number of his subjects, and all eyes are now towards William and his wife Mary, who is our poor king's daughter. We must have liberty of conscience in our land and that James is trying to take from us."

But there was no time for prolonged explanations. The ships drew near and presently the Prince and his soldiers landed. Four thousand five hundred cavalry and eleven thousand foot soldiers with large military stores. Among these men were a large number of French officers,

Huguenots who having been forced to leave their own land had joined the Prince of Orange. One of these was René de Vere.

After he had been in England a few weeks, he found an opportunity of sending a letter to his sister Catherine, whom he had left in Holland in attendance on the Princess of Orange, who hoped to join her husband as soon as England was in a more settled condition.

René wrote as follows:

Westminster, January 1689.

" My dearest sister,

I find that our Prince is sending an envoy to Holland with letters to his wife, and I have asked permission to send one to you, as I know you will be anxious to hear how I am faring.

" We had a good voyage, I am thankful to say. You can imagine my feelings as we sighted the coast of France, my still loved country. I thought of our dear father, so lonely in his old age. How I wish we could persuade him to join us. At length we left the coast of France behind us and sighted the English shores, sailing along towards the west. Night fell then and when day dawned we had lost sight of land and we wondered if we had passed out of the English Channel, but at three in the afternoon we again saw land, and found we were still holding the same course. One of the officers, who knew the coast, said we were making for Plymouth, but the wind shifted and under a brilliant sky we sailed into Tor Bay and landed at a little fishing village by the name of Brixham. Our landing was a long tedious affair, with all our troops and baggage. The village folk seemed scared, for I understand, that in the west of England the people suffered such terrible punishment for joining the rebellion under the Duke of Monmouth, that they are naturally terrified at incurring the displeasure of the king.

It is not easy for these simple country people to understand we are here by the direct and urgent invitation of the nation, including the nobility and the commoners, to set the king's daughter and son-in-law on the throne and bring in a righteous rule.

"However they are learning now to trust us, but that first day with the exception of the gentry, all stood aloof. Well, we started the next day along villainous roads to march to Exeter. I should like sometime Catherine, to take you to Devon and show you some of the beauty of the country. It reminds me of Normandy. We passed inland, leaving Tor Bay, the sea deep blue, the coves and beaches many of them gleaming white, the cliffs are red, a glorious combination of colouring. We climbed a long hill, a mere muddy track where our horses and men were up to their knees in mud, down hill again to a little village of the name of Cockington, these English names are queer, there we found a forge and some of the horses were re-shod. Towards evening we reached a fine mansion known as Forde House. There our Prince and many of his officers found shelter for the night. I cannot say they were exactly welcomed, for the owner of the house did not even appear. I suppose he wanted to be on the safe side whatever happened. A number of us pressed on another mile and I found a good coffee house in Newton Abbot and slept there, the men finding billets in the cottages. It was a packed town that night, and like locusts, we devoured all the food the towns-folk had, but they were cheerful, for we all paid well for what we had.

"Next morning our Prince came along and there by the little church which stands immediately outside the coffee house where I slept, Prince William was proclaimed. Then we went on and reaching a farmhouse a mile out, William held his first Parliament in England.

"So we continued until we reached Exeter. I was

glad to be in that city, for many of our countrymen have settled there and we French Protestants got a warm welcome. Our leader decided we must all get a rest so we remained six days, then on again to Reading, there King James' army made a faint show of resistance, but a handful of our men put them to flight, led, by the way, by a Huguenot officer Colonel Marouit. Not another shot was fired all the way, and we arrived in London where our Prince was splendidly received as the nation's deliverer.

"The unhappy King James started off in disguise to flee, reaching Sheerness, some fisherman discovered who he was and seized him, sending him back to London. However our Prince had no desire to retain him or punish him, the Prince having promised his wife, Princess Mary, that her father should not be harmed. So when the King asked for permission to retire to Rochester it was given, and from thence he embarked secretly in a frigate and got to France. So ends this unhappy reign and now things are hastening on for the coronation. Your lady, the Princess Mary, will be receiving letters at the same time as you get this, directing her to come at once to England, so dearest Catherine I shall hope to see you before long, as you will come in her retinue. Tell Jacqueline she will find many of her own people here. There are several Huguenot churches. I worshipped in one in Threadneedle Street last Sunday and had a good time. A large number gather to worship there. I am told that in one month four hundred and ninety seven members were received into fellowship, all of whom had, under the force of terror in our land, pretended to abandoned the faith. Poor souls one cannot judge them, we were spared the temptation. Now there is a great humility about them and much earnest service.

"I must draw this letter to a close now, for all communications have to be ready to-day, Prince William's messenger being about to start. God have you in His keeping dear sister, and give you a safe journey. With affectionate commendations,

Your loving brother, René."

Catherine de Vere was delighted to receive her brother's letter, she read it eagerly and would probably have perused it a second time, but a summons came to attend her royal mistress. The Princess Mary was as pleased at getting her husband's letter as Catherine had been at receiving hers. The Princess, a gentle, amiable lady, devoted to her husband, was eager to get the packing done and start as soon as possible for England, so her ladies were all busy at once, some pleased at the change, others a little doubtful as to what might be involved.

Catherine was tremendously excited at the thought of joining her brother. At the first opportunity she told Jacqueline of their plans.

"England!" Jacqueline said, her face flushing.

"Yes, do you like the idea?"

"Oh yes. I was wondering whether we should be likely to find M. and Madame Durand."

"Durand," Catherine repeated wonderingly. Then she remembered and said: "Oh yes, your father's late employer. You would like to see them?"

"Very much indeed. Madame Durand and Mademoiselle Marie were always kind to us. I expect if they got safely to England they have often wondered what became of us, you see father had promised to join his master in England. I should like to be able to tell them about mother, and about father and Pierre too, they will be so sorry.

"Yes I am sure they will be," Catherine said.

"I do so wonder if father and Pierre are still alive? Somehow it seems so much easier to bear the loss of mother, because I know she is at rest, but the uncertainty about the others is hard to bear. I think, I think, so often about them."

Jacqueline's eyes filled with tears. Catherine put her hand on the girl's shoulder with a sympathetic gesture.

"We will try and find the Durands, Jacqueline. Do you remember which town they were going to."

Jacqueline could not recall it.

"Father knew the name, and I did hear it, but I have forgotten.

"Tell me about the Durands," Catherine said, with the idea in her mind of turning Jacqueline's thoughts away from her lover and father.

The two were busily engaged in packing as they talked. So Jacqueline told her mistress of André, Ninon, and of Mademoiselle Marie.

"André was about fourteen at that dreadful time four years ago, he must be a man now and little Ninon is I suppose twelve," Jacqueline said.

"And is Marie an elder sister ?"

"Oh no. She is M. Durand's younger sister, she is aunt to André and Ninon. Such a sweet lady."

The two might have gone on talking for some time but a matronly Dutch lady bustled in. The Mistress of the Robes kept a firm hand over the young ladies in waiting at the court.

She gave orders that Mademoiselle Catherine must get to bed early as they would be starting at dawn next morning. Was the packing finished ?

Finding it was almost done, the good lady left the girls to complete the task and get to bed.

Chapter XXX

A VISIT TO LONDON

GASTON DURAND approached his wife one day with a proposal. He was smiling blandly and looking as though he were immensely pleased with the idea he had in his mind, and which he was about to reveal to his wife.

"Rachelle, my dear, I think it will be necessary for me to go to London on business. You know I am getting a good many orders for our paduasoys, lustings, brocades and tabinets and I should like to interview some who are sending orders, and get into touch with others who might become customers. In some cases I feel I am not getting a fair price and a conference of business men, if arranged, might do much to right the difficulty,"

"Yes dear. I expect you are wise to go. We shall miss you greatly while you are away and my prayers for your safety will ascend to the throne of grace frequently. One hears such tales of highwaymen now-a-days, travel is so dangerous."

"Not too bad, dearest," Gaston said smiling as he spoke. "The coaches get through in safety most times. But what would you say if I suggested your coming with me? You have been in this one spot now for four years and I think a little change would be beneficial to you. I need not give all my time to business, we can combine pleasure with it. I should like myself to see some of the sights of London. It is a wonderful city, I have read much about it."

Gaston paused and his wife gasped in astonishment.

"My dear! How can I leave home? Who will look after the children?

"They are not little children now Rachelle, but I have thought of that. Marie will be delighted to have Ninon and Leonie for a week or two, and I am thinking André could pay that long promised visit to Captain and Mistress Hopkins at Rye. Last time our old friend was here he said how much he would like André to stay with them. I think having lost his boy in that terrible rebellion has given him a tender heart towards all lads. André will like the change. We shall feel happy about the young folk and fortunately my work-people are reliable, under our good foreman, all will go on as if I were at home."

Rachelle still hesitated. Gaston continued: "You would like to come with me, dear heart?"

"Yes indeed. But a mother gets in the way of thinking she is indispensable. Yes, I will come Gaston, when do you wish to start?"

"Well now that I know you are willing, I will book our seats in the coach for one day next week. That will give you time to get ready."

"Yes, my clothes and yours are in order, so I shall not need much time to pack the carpet bag."

Gaston laughed. "Everything you have charge of, is always in order, dearest. We must tell Ninon and Leonie, they will be amazed at the thought of going away from home."

"And André too. What a joy the dear boy is, we can trust him to go away by himself and feel that he will be wise."

"That is so, when I see how foolish and headstrong some lads of his age are, I cannot but be thankful for our boy. Rachelle have you noticed how his devotion to Leonie seems to deepen?"

Rachelle Durand sighed.

"Yes I do see it I sometimes feel troubled about it. Leonie has such a flippant disposition and André is so intense and deep. But there, she is but a child still, it will be another eight years before we need think seriously of this."

"Girls frequently marry at fifteen years of age, Rachelle, and I believe André is determined to wait for her. He hinted as much to me the other day. The trouble to my mind is that André is a sincere Christian and so far poor little Leonie is not willing to open her heart to the Lord."

"I am glad you have the dear boy's confidence Gaston. We can only wait and pray. Did you say anything to Marie about the girls coming to her?"

"Yes I did, before I approached you on the subject, I thought I'd like to have some suggestion to make to you which would help you to decide. She and John are pleased at the idea and I'm sure Lawrence and Lovedy will be. What a contrast that home is now from what it was when first we knew it. John so happy, Lawrence's face absolutely changed, the old sullen look gone and his countenance steadily cheerful, and as for little Lovedy, an old acquaintance would scarcely know her. It was a pretty sight, I thought, when I was there last week, to see the child holding her little stepbrother in such a motherly fashion. He is a beautiful child and I tell John and Marie that I feel flattered that they have decided to call him Gaston after me."

"And how did you find old Mrs. Giles?" Rachelle asked.

"Failing rapidly. From the day of John's marriage when the old lady gave up the management of the home, she has weakened."

"Poor old soul. She was really getting frail before that, and she knew it, and that was one reason why she was so difficult, she hated to feel her power was waning. Have you ever had any talk with her on spiritual matters?"

"I have tried to more than once, Rachelle, but she is not easy to reach. She will converse with me on every other subject, she is keen on politics, history, affairs of nations, but directly I speak of my Master and His salvation she is silent. So I can only give the message and leave it."

"It seems remarkable that with such a mother, and such an upbringing, that John should be a sincere Christian."

"Yes, but he seems to have learnt from an old servant when he was a child, and his simple faith has grown since his contact with Marie."

"Ah! Who would not? Dear Marie is one of God's best, so quiet and unassuming, but so full of faith and good works."

Presently Rachelle continued: "You referred just now to that rebellion under Monmouth, is it safe for us to go to London now that there is a rising again under the Prince of Orange. Shall we not find there is much unrest?"

"No fear of that. 'The Public Intelligencer' came yesterday, and I sat up rather late reading it. It seems that William has been well received."

Gaston rose from his seat and fetched the paper saying: "Let me read it to you. 'A declaration has been made, that King James having endeavoured to subvert the constitution of the kingdom by breaking the original contract between king and people, and by the advice of Jesuits and other wicked persons having violated the fundamental laws and having withdrawn himself out of the kingdom has thereby abdicated the government and that the throne has become vacant. In consequence of this, and after a long debate in the House, the crown has been tendered to William and Mary who have accepted the offer and are now on the throne and at present are very popular with the people.'"

"Ah well, I hope this will turn out for the best. I can never forget how much we owe to this land and what a haven it has been to us."

Gaston agreed with his wife, as indeed he had occasion to do.

Then Rachelle said: "I will now tell Ninon and Leonie what we are planning for them. It will be a surprise."

Gaston went off to the workroom and Rachelle called the girls.

They were delighted at the prospect of visiting Aunt Marie.

"We shall be able to help take care of the dear little baby," Ninon said.

Leonie looked thoughtful. Suddenly a gleam of mischief twinkled in her eyes, and she exclaimed: "Ninon, you can nurse the baby, I am going to play with Lawrence."

Ninon flushed. "Lawrence is a big boy, Leonie, he will not want to play with a little girl like you. He and I have long serious talks together, we don't play."

Leonie stamped her foot. "He will want to play with me, if I wish it. All the boys like playing with me. See how much André does."

Ninon could not deny this, and her face grew stormy. Her mother intervened. "That will do girls. I hope you will both have a happy time and not be quarrelsome. Leonie you can go with Betsy to the shops, she is going to do some errands. Ninon, you and I will go to the garden. It is such a fine day we can put in a bit of work."

Rachelle had longed so much for a garden and as it was impossible to have one around the house, surrounded, as it was by the road, other houses and the river, Gaston had purchased a piece of land a little distance out, and there Rachelle was able to grow cabbages, celery, carrots and flowers of all sorts. It gave her much pleasure and her English neighbours were following her example, consequently growing vegetables was becoming usual.

Madame Durand and Ninon walked in silence for a time. Ninon's face was troubled. Her mother waited, she knew presently her daughter would confide in her and she was not disappointed, Ninon said with a sigh: "I wish I could be good."

"Do you dear? I am glad you have that desire."

"Mother, I do try not to be jealous of Leonie, but—but it comes up again and again in my heart. She wants everything."

They had reached the garden now, and Madame Durand suggested that they should sit down on a seat and have a talk. Gaston and André had made a rustic bench and Madame Durand often rested there between her labours.

"Ninon dear, when you feel those jealous feelings rising and do not give way to them, that is victory. I have noticed several times that you have conquered the enemy and I am thankful for that, but I know what it is you desire, that is, a complete deliverance in your heart, so that you do not feel the jealousy rising within.

"I do Mother and I pray that I might, but it's very difficult."

Ninon again sighed.

"Yes dear, the natural tendency to sin is indeed terrible I know, and it is too strong for you. You fight, but you cannot entirely overcome."

"Then there is no hope for me Mother?" Ninon asked.

"Indeed there is, but not in your own strength. You believe that Jesus died for your sins don't you?

"Yes. I believe He died for me."

"Then Ninon listen, He rose again and He lives to save you. The Bible says in the epistle to the Romans, 'If when we were enemies we were reconciled to God by the death of His Son, much more being reconciled we shall be saved by His life.' It is Jesus Himself dwelling in your heart by faith Who can save you to the uttermost."

Ninon was very quiet. Presently she said: "Mother you know that, don't you?"

"Yes dear. I will tell you a secret, something I have never told anyone. I used to be jealous of Aunt Marie. I did not like your father being so fond of her and I did not want her to live with us. But Jesus came into my heart and he conquered there."

'Oh Mother!" Ninon said in amazement. Then she added: "Thank you for telling me. I know how you love Aunt Marie now."

"Yes dear I do."

In the days that followed Madame Durand noticed a great difference in Ninon and years afterwards she told her mother that the words, 'Jesus saves by His life,' had taken hold of her and that she often whispered to herself, 'Jesus saves' and found it true.

That evening when Leonie was in bed, Madame Durand went to kiss her "Good-night." Leonie was very affectionate. She said: "You do love me lots, don't you, Mother?" Her pretty little face was dimpling with an attractive smile.

"Yes darling I do, but it grieves me very much when I see you conceited and selfish." Leonie pouted and then as if to change the conversation said: "I'm not really your little girl, am I?"

"Not my little daughter, dear. I have always told you how André found you wandering in a lane and afterwards we heard that your parents had given their lives for Christ's sake."

"Yes I know. Everybody calls me Leonie Durand but that is not my name."

"Your name is Furneaux, dear."

"Mother, have I any relations in France?"

"I don't know at all, Leonie."

"Well when I am big I'm going to France to find out. Were my father and mother rich people?"

"I think perhaps they were, for the man who knew you, and told us your name, said your people lived in a castle."

"That castle belongs to me now, doesn't it? I want to find out, I'm going to France one day."

"Well dearie, there is lots of time to think about that. You are still a little girl. You must remember your people were Huguenots and their rights are not acknowledged in France. Most likely the government has taken all that belonged to your parents. I want you to forget all this and just be my happy little girl. We love you and feel that God gave you to us, so we shall always take care of you."

Leonie flung her arms around her adopted mother's neck, saying: "I am glad I belong to you, Mother."

Madame Durand returned the embrace and then said: "I wish my Leonie belonged to Jesus Christ. Dear, when are you going to give your heart to Jesus?"

Leonie looked grave for a moment, then she brightened and said: "I will one day, Mother, when I am old. I need not think about it yet."

Madame Durand sighed. Leonie was so lighthearted, she wondered if it would be only through trouble and suffering that she would be touched and would seek the Saviour. Madame Durand feared it might be so, she had a presentiment that difficulties would come, and only thus would Leonie find salvation.

She kissed the child, said "Good-night" and left her.

Leonie nestling down in her bed whispered to herself: "Anyhow I am going to France as soon as I'm big enough. I want to find things out."

Chapter XXXI

A HAPPY MEETING

WHEN Pierre Benoit found himself at last in England, he felt extremely lonely. The boat in which he had made the voyage called at Rye, and Pierre understanding from the captain that this was England, decided to go no further. He walked away from the harbour, looking at the faces of the people he met, hoping he would see someone who looked French. But every one he came across appeared so typically British that he began to feel a sense of despair. Then he chided himself. Had he not been praying for guidance? Had he not received a wonderful deliverance? God would complete that which he had begun.

Faith triumphed once again in his heart. He decided to speak to the next person he met, and ask about an Inn where he could lodge.

A good-natured looking woman came in sight. Pierre spoke to her but alas! he could not speak English, she knew no French.

Pierre tried signs, the woman shouted, evidently thinking her words would convey more meaning if spoken in a loud tone. She shook her head at last in despair and Pierre was about to move away, when a young man came around a corner, whistling lightheartedly.

As he advanced he paused, he caught the sound of a few French words. Ah, here was someone from his own land. He hastened on, eager to render assistance.

It was André Durand who was paying his visit to Captain Hopkins and his wife. His sympathies were stirred at the need of a fellow countryman unable to make himself understood.

He lifted his cap and greeted Pierre in French. Pierre exclaimed excitedly. To hear his native tongue was a joy indeed. He made known his need of somewhere to stay and André suggested an Inn near by, adding: " Can I do anything to help you sir ? "

As he spoke and looked at Pierre, memory stirred in his mind, he had a strange sense of having known this man in the past and yet he knew not the man's name nor where he had seen him. This was no matter for surprise for Pierre had changed greatly, the years of suffering as a galley slave had left their mark. He looked much older than his years. André too had grown from boyhood to young manhood, so it was not to be wondered at that neither recognised the other.

But André having a feeling that he had met the man before, decided to keep in touch with him and offered to accompany him to the Inn, and make arrangements with the landlord for Pierre's visit.

This offer Pierre accepted gladly, and as they went they talked. André asked if Pierre meant to stay long in Rye adding: " I shall be here a day or two longer so if I can be of any help to you I shall be delighted."

" Thank you Master. I shall be glad of your aid. I know not how to set about my quest. I am seeking a friend who I believe is in this country, and I should like to find my old master who would probably give me work. He and his family came to England some four or five years ago. I am trusting the Lord to guide me. He has wrought a wonderful deliverance for me from the galleys and He will not forsake me now."

" Ah, you belong to the Saviour," André said, " I am doubly pleased to help you, now I know that. I am staying with Captain Hopkins at the sign of 'The Oak Leaf.' My name is André Durand. I—"

Pierre gave a shout of joy. " Why Master André, this is good. Don't you know me ? I'm Pierre Benoit."

André stared at his companion. " Why, of course I remember you Pierre, but I did not know you at first. I have that little carved cherry stone you did for me when I was about six years old. I have always kept it. Where have you been all these years ? Father expected you would arrive in England ere this, for he felt sure your mother could not live long, and then he knew you meant to follow us. And the Goyers, what became of them ? "

" Well Master André, to answer your first question, I was taken and sent to the galleys. I must tell you of my wonderful deliverance some day. And the Goyers, poor Mistress Goyer was killed by the soldiers, her husband went with me to the galleys and died after a year of toil. And Jacqueline, you remember Jacqueline ? "

" Oh yes. Pretty Jacqueline with the lovely hair. I do hope she escaped."

" She was taken to a convent, but like myself she had a wonderful deliverance. I don't know many of the details of her escape, I went to the convent and found out from a village woman that Jacqueline had been taken away, and the woman understood that she had gone to England so I am come here to seek for her."

André was extremely interested.

" We must find her," he said heartily," but first you must come with me when I return to my home in Canterbury. Father and Mother will welcome you I know and father will advise you as to how best to seek Jacqueline. I am sure now that you need not go to the Inn, Pierre. My hostess, Mistress Hopkins will be pleased to see any friend of mine."

" I do not want to intrude, Master André " Pierre said, but André insisted and found he was right in thinking

Mistress Hopkins would gladly entertain André's fellow countryman.

Pierre did not need any persuasion to accompany André to Canterbury, when he left Rye in a few days time.

Meanwhile M. and Madame Durand were spending pleasant days in London.

William and Mary had been crowned in Westminster Abbey and Londoners were having a gay and peaceful time. Trade was flourishing, and M. Durand found himself sought after by the merchants, as he had brought samples of uncommon silks to exhibit. France had been for long the leader in fashion and now that the same goods were being made in England, the refugees found a ready sale for all their produce.

One day he came into the room where his wife was sitting, looking immensely pleased.

"My dear, you will be interested in what I have to tell you. Master Pelon, the merchant, with whom I have been dealing for some time, supplies some of the Court ladies with material for their gowns, and he wishes me to accompany him to the Palace with my samples, as Queen Mary and several of her ladies require to replenish their wardrobes. Master Pelon thinks they will be pleased with my goods."

"That is interesting, Gaston," Rachelle replied. "I should think they certainly ought to be pleased, for nowhere could one find better goods than yours."

Gaston laughed. "I hope they will be of your opinion, my dearest. I wish you could accompany me to the Palace."

"My dear, I should be a sparrow among the peacocks. You will be able to tell me all about it on your return. When do you go?"

"To-morrow morning. Meanwhile we can spend to-day sight-seeing. Put on your bonnet and cloak and come out."

Next morning Rachelle said to her husband as he went off: "Now take note of everything. I shall want a full account."

But such a surprising incident took place, on this the occasion of Gaston's visit to the royal palace, that Rachelle forgot for some time to ask what the Queen was like and what the ladies in waiting wore.

Gaston and his guide had finished their interview and were departing well satisfied with the reception that had been given to their goods.

They had been received in an upstairs room and Gaston was about to descend the staircase, when he heard a little scream and a figure rushed towards him, exclaiming "M. Durand! M. Durand! Oh it is you!"

Gaston looked in surprise at the girl who thus addressed him, then he too exclaimed: "Why it is Jacqueline Goyer! My child how came you here in the palace?"

"I am with my mistress sir, Mademoiselle Catherine de Vere, she is one of the Queen's ladies. Oh, I am glad to see you sir. I was just crossing the corridor and I caught a glimpse of you. I knew you at once. Will you come and see my mistress? I have told her about you and she will be pleased to see you. She is of 'the faith' sir."

"Ah that is good news, Jacqueline."

M. Durand turned to Master Pelon who was waiting for him. "If you will excuse me sir, I would like to linger awhile and see this lady, Mademoiselle de Vere. Will this afternoon do for me to visit you in your office?"

"Certainly, certainly, M. Durand. We can settle out business then."

So M. Durand accompanied Jacqueline to her mistress'

apartments. She led him into a small room saying: " Will you sit here please, while I find out if Mademoiselle can see you, she is not in attendance on the Queen this morning, so I think it will be all right."

Presently she returned and reported that Mademoiselle de Vere would see M. Durand.

Much conversation followed and M. Durand heard of Jacqueline's time in the convent; of Catherine's conversion; of their escape to Holland and their journey to England.

Presently M. Durand said: " I wonder Mademoiselle whether you could spare Jacqueline to accompany us when we return to Canterbury next week. It would give my wife much pleasure to have her for a short visit, and Jacqueline will like to see my children and sister whom she knew well in the old days in France."

Catherine de Vere gave her consent and Jacqueline's cup of joy was almost full.

CHAPTER XXXII

THE LOVERS

THE day before the Durands were to leave for home M. Durand fetched Jacqueline from the palace. The meeting between Madame and Jacqueline was very moving. Both shed tears, for so much had taken place since they last met, that it was only natural that there should be tears of joy and sorrow. Rachelle Durand could not but feel full of sympathy with the girl who had gone through so much suffering, and had come out unscathed in her faith and love for the Master.

They had a great deal to talk about, and Jacqueline confided in Madame Durand that, although she loved her mistress, she did not like the life in London, nor those with whom she was obliged to associate, the other maids of the ladies-in-waiting. Madame Durand wondered whether Mademoiselle de Vere would be willing to let Jacqueline remain with them in Canterbury, but of this at the moment she said nothing.

When the little party reached home they found André had not yet arrived, but they were not surprised for M. Durand had given him freedom to decide for himself exactly how long his holiday should last. However, next day, when Ninon and Leonie, who had returned from a pleasant visit at the farm, had taken Jacqueline to see the Cathedral, André arrived, and not only André but to Gaston and Rachelle's amazement and pleasure, Pierre Benoit also.

Rachelle recalled what had, for a time, escaped her memory, that in the old days before they had left France, Jacqueline and Pierre had been affianced.

She was delighted at the remembrance, and as soon as she could take her husband on one side, she reminded him of this and asked: " Shall I tell Pierre that Jacqueline is here, or shall I just let it be a surprise ? "

Gaston laughed. " Oh you women ! How you love a romance. Better tell him I think, he looks to me as though he has passed through stress and strain. A shock, albeit it is a pleasant one, would not be good for him."

So Madame Durand tactfully led the conversation around to the Goyers and heard with grief of the death of Jacques and Colette.

Then she asked for Jacqueline and Pierre told her what he had found out, adding: " I must now seek her, if it be through the length and breadth of the land."

" Your search need not be a long one, Pierre," Madame said.

" What do you mean Madame ? "

Pierre was quickly agitated and Madame hastened to say: " Pierre, Jacqueline is here. She is out just at the moment with the girls. We found her in London only a few days ago and brought her home with us."

" Is she well ? Has she suffered ? "

" She looks the picture of health and bonnier than ever. She did have a bad time in the convent, but she has been well cared for by Mademoiselle de Vere. Jacqueline was the means of her young mistress' conversion and the two are deeply attached to one another."

Pierre buried his face in his hands. He was unable to speak for a few moments, emotion overcame him.

Presently he said: " Please excuse me, Madame. The good news coming so unexpectedly seemed to knock me over. To think I shall see my little girl after all these hopeless years. Truly the Lord has done great things for me. There I was, a helpless galley slave, and now delivered and given my heart's desire."

" Yes indeed. Yours must be a wonderful story

Pierre. By-and-bye we must hear all about it, but now I see the girls approaching; you stay here and I will send Jacqueline to you. Dearie me, what a surprise it will be to her."

Madame Durand met the girls at the door. " My dear, there is an old friend of ours in the sitting-room. You will be glad to see him," she said to Jacqueline.

The colour came and went in Jacqueline's face. One name rose to her lips, but she checked herself thinking of course that cannot be.

Rachelle Durand was all smiles. " Go and see, my dear. No Leonie, don't go with her," she added as Leonie was about to follow Jacqueline.

Jacqueline walked into the room and her face was blank for she only saw a worn-looking man of middle age. She held out her hand politely.

" Good morning, Madame tells me you wished to see me."

Pierre took a step forward, holding out his arms.

" My little Jacqueline, don't you know your Pierre ? "

Ah ! the face had changed, the shoulders were bowed, but the voice, the loved voice was the same.

With a little cry, Jacqueline fell into those outstretched arms.

" Pierre, Pierre," was all she could say. Then she burst into tears, but Pierre knew how to comfort her.

After a time he said: " Jacqueline look at me. I'm not what I was when we parted. Can you still love a man so worn and bent as I am ? "

" Pierre how can you ask ? I am proud of all the signs that show you suffered for Christ's sake. And I am going to take care of you. But oh dear, what will my mistress say ? I wonder if she will spare me. I had forgotten her for the moment."

Pierre's lips took a firm line.

" We are not going to be separated, my little one. I

can work at my trade. I am sure M. and Madame Durand will advise us and I shall make a home for you."

Gaston and Rachelle Durand entered heartily into the plans. Gaston was only too pleased to engage Pierre as his workman. One day after a few weeks had passed, Pierre and Jacqueline were married, and prepared to settle in Canterbury.

However Mademoiselle de Vere had other ideas. She and her brother did not like court life and had taken a house in Surrey, where, to their great joy, their father decided to join them, having succeeded in getting a good sale for his property in France. Now Catherine suggested that Pierre and Jacqueline should come to them. There was work for Pierre in the garden and Jacqueline could still be her maid. A nice little house in the grounds was ready for them.

When the offer came to the Benoits, they held a consultation with the Durands and finally decided that this plan was best. An outdoor life would suit Pierre, and Jacqueline was so fond of Mademoiselle de Vere that she had felt grieved at being separated from her mistress.

So although sorry to leave the Durands, Pierre and Jacqueline went off to Surrey. Gradually Pierre regained his health and looked younger, while Jacqueline, with happiness and love surrounding her, grew sweeter than ever.

Neither of them would ever forget the time of trouble through which they had passed, and always was there a song of praise in their hearts to God for His wonderful deliverance.

Chapter XXXIII

SEVEN YEARS LATER

ANDRE DURAND and his father were walking together on the footpath by the river Stour. They had been discussing business matters, both were pleased to know that they were prospering.

M. Durand remarked: "When I look back to that time eleven years ago, when with fearful hearts your mother and I left our land, our home, our flourishing business for Christ's sake, I realise how little need there was for our fears. God has protected and guided, given us safety and all that we need in the land of our adoption. I can echo the words of the Holy Book, 'say to them that are of a fearful heart fear not.' Eleven years ago André, and you were only a lad, now you are twenty-five, Ninon a young woman betrothed to our good friend Lawrence, I suppose they will be getting married next year, and even our little Leonie beginning to think herself grown up. By-the-bye André, when are you going to think about getting married. I was a father before I was your age. I believe in early marriages providing the man can maintain his wife without undue anxiety. It's time you gave your mind to the matter, my son."

"I've done that for many a year, sir."

"Indeed André. Then why not go farther and put your thoughts into action."

"Well father I have been delaying because of Leonie's youth."

Gaston Durand frowned slightly.

He feared this, but had been determined to ignore the danger. "Well to be sure. There was a time when I thought that might be so, but lately I had hoped you cared for her more as a big brother. I cannot feel that Leonie will make you a suitable wife, my son. She is so lighthearted, and you are inclined to gravity, and more than that, there is one great barrier. You are a servant of the Lord Jesus Christ, our Master, and our dear little Leonie has not made any profession of conversion."

"I know Father, but surely if she becomes my wife I shall be able to win her."

"No my lad, that is an argument from the enemy of our souls. Marry only in the Lord, is the direction given us in the Word. Much as I should like to see you happily settled, I would rather you should walk through life alone, than be united to one who would hinder you in your loyalty to Christ."

André was about to reply but his father continued: "Much as I love Leonie I cannot but see that she loves the things of this world. She is bored by the Sunday services. I fear when she is old enough to choose for herself, it will be the world, unless our prayers are answered speedily and she is brought into the fold of the Good Shepherd."

André sighed. There was a struggle going on in his heart. The two walked in silence. Gaston Durand was praying for his son. When they reached home Gaston put his hand on his son's shoulder saying: "You have my sympathy my boy. I know you are suffering, and there is no hurt like wounded love. Would I could bear it for you."

André gripped his father's hand but he could not speak. The battle must be fought alone.

Next day Leonie and Ninon were out together and passing the cathedral, Leonie said: "Do let us go in. We need not be back for another hour."

Both girls loved roaming round the building, ever discovering fresh beauties. Ninon agreed readily and together they made a leisurely tour. There were few people in the cathedral at the moment; two men, one middle-aged, the other young, were standing before the tomb of the Black Prince as Leonie and Ninon came in that direction.

Leonie gave Ninon a touch and whispered: "French, I feel sure."

Ninon nodded and would have passed on, but Leonie lingered, her eyes sparkling with interest.

Again she whispered to Ninon. "Isn't that young man handsome ?"

"Ye-s in a way, but I think he has a cruel scornful expression. I should not want to know him," was Ninon's reply ; then she unconsciously raised her voice: "Come on Leonie, we must be going home."

Evidently her words were heard by the older man. He turned and looked at the girls and as he did so he threw up his hand with a gesture of astonishment. He stepped forward.

"Excuse me Mademoiselle, what is your name ?"

"Leonie Furneaux," Leonie replied briefly.

"But, but I cannot understand. Leonie Furneaux, my little daughter was killed in France eleven years ago, and yet you are the image of my dear, dead wife who was also killed then. And your name ? Tell me, tell me who are you ?"

"I am Leonie Furneaux. I was brought to England from France by M. Durand, who found me wandering in a lane and adopted me when I was four."

Ninon was amazed at Leonie's quick response to the questioner. She had no idea how often Leonie had rehearsed a scene something like this, in her day dreams. Only Leonie had always thought of it as taking place in France, where she was determined to go as soon as she was old enough.

"This is marvellous, thrilling, wonderful !"

The Frenchman was greatly excited. He turned to the younger man saying: "Henri, this must be my child whom I thought was killed. My child! My daughter! The image of my dear wife!"

Henri interrupted the flow. "Sir, we shall want proofs."

"Proofs! The likeness, the name, the circumstance! Do not be so cold-blooded. Leonie come with me. Come back to France."

Ninon here interposed. "Sir, will you come home with us? My father, who has brought Leonie up, will want to know if your claim is a true one."

"Ah yes. Your parents. I must see them and thank them for the care they have taken of my child. Come Leonie, take my hand, I am afraid you will vanish into thin air. Come Henri, we will lose no time in seeing these good people and claiming our dear one."

Henri did not look well pleased. Leonie's face was flushed with excitement, her eyes sparkled. Here was an adventure to break the monotony of her existence. Ninon was grave. It was all so sudden, so unexpected, would her parents be pleased? She thought not.

Together they hastened home. Ninon asked the visitors to be seated in a small room near the door saying: "I will tell my father and mother of your arrival sir. I would like to prepare them to meet you by making known what you have said."

M. Furneaux could scarce restrain his impatience, but he consented to sit down and wait a few moments.

Meanwhile Leonie had dashed to the upstairs room where M. and Madame Durand were seated, André also being with them.

"Mother, mother, I've found my own father. He's here. Oh isn't it wonderful?"

Ninon followed almost immediately and gave a more lucid account of what had happened. All three listeners were astonished. André's face grew very grave. Rachelle Durand was looking white and distressed.

" Ninon, bring the gentleman up " M. Durand said after a moment or two.

They were all surprised to see two gentlemen follow Ninon into the room. They thought that Leonie must have had a brother, yet she had never referred to one, although she had in the early days spoken of mother, father and nurse.

Soon they understood. Henri had been adopted by M. Furneaux when he found himself without wife or child. Rachelle produced the little garments Leonie had worn when they had found her. M. Furneaux at once recognised a locket which had hung around the child's neck and professed himself perfectly satisfied that Leonie was his daughter, hastening to add: " I must take her home with me when I return."

M. Durand interrupted the conversation. " I must be satisfied first, sir, that you are Leonie's father before I permit her to accompany you to France. The conviction must be on both sides. I understood that her father was killed at the same time as her mother. If I had thought otherwise I should have ere this made some effort to find you."

M. Furneaux grew very red in the face.

" I was in Switzerland at the time and so escaped. Is not my word sufficient ? I am not accustomed to be doubted."

" I am sorry sir, but we have cared for Leonie all these years and she is dear to us, we must be sure that you have a right to her."

M. Furneaux waved his hands excitedly. He was much annoyed, but Henri quieted him.

" Father the gentleman is right. We might easily be impostors seeking to get hold of the girl for no good purpose."

" How can I prove my right ? " Ah, I have it ! I am staying at ' The Fountain ' and I have with me a small painting of Leonie done by a famous painter only a few weeks before I lost her. You will recognise her and also see the child in the picture is wearing the very same necklace and locket which we have here, and which you have kept as a sign by which she might be known. Henri, go at once to our rooms and fetch the picture. I have always taken it with me on every journey, for I assure you I was deeply attached to my little daughter. That will convince you I think sir, that I am the father of Leonie."

Henri obeyed and soon returned with the picture. Gaston and Rachelle Durand were both convinced. It was a picture of Leonie as they first knew her and round her neck hung the little chain and locket which M. Furneaux now held in his hand.

" Leonie " Gaston Durand said turning to the girl " is it your wish to go with your father ? You are old enough to decide for yourself. You will always, dear child, have a place in our hearts and a welcome in our home, but we must now waive our claim on you."

Leonie's expressive face showed signs of conflicting emotions. She flushed, paled and trembled. But before she could reply M. Furneaux exclaimed: " My child, my daughter, I have mourned for you all these years, lonely years indeed. Am I still to be bereaved ? Come to your home, there gaiety and happy days await you. Henri and I will unite in making your life a round of pleasure. Come, be the solace of my old age. These good people, to whom I owe an eternal debt of gratitude which I can never repay, have their own son and daughter. Come with me, my angel."

Tears stood in M. Furneaux' eyes and Leonie did not resist his appeal. Indeed she had no wish to do so. The gaiety suggested thrilled her, and she said: " Of course I must go with you, Father."

Then she turned to Madame Durand: "Mother, mother, you would not hold me back."

Rachelle Durand's face was very sad, but she spoke quietly: "No dear. I will not hold you from your parent, but dear, remember there will always be a home here for you. We have loved you for eleven years and our love is not a thing to wither at the first cold blast."

"Oh mother, mother," Leonie cried and flung herself into Rachelle's arms with a little sob.

M. Furneaux rose. "We need not prolong this scene," he said stiffly. "I thank you all sincerely for what you have done for my child. Now, Henri and I will return to the 'Fountain Inn' where we are staying. We are remaining five days longer and I shall be grateful to you Madame if you will have my daughter ready to accompany me to France at the expiration of those days. She need only take clothes sufficient for her journey. We shall visit Paris on our way home and her wardrobe can be replenished. I will call again before I leave for further conversation. Come Henri."

So the two departed leaving the family, formerly so tranquil, feeling as though an earthquake had taken place in their midst.

Chapter XXXIV

ANDRE'S VICTORY

IN the days that followed Leonie became very excited. The thought of travelling, the promise of new clothes, the novelty of an unknown home all appealed to her giddy, pleasure loving heart. M. Furneaux came each day to see her, and told her of all he meant to do for her. He had an interview with Gaston Durand and offered to pay for the maintenance of his child. Gaston absolutely refused to receive compensation in any way.

"We have loved the child and treated her as our own," he said simply but firmly. And that ended the matter.

In a talk with Rachelle, M. Furneaux told her that he intended that Henri and Leonie should marry as soon as Leonie was a little older.

"They will be betrothed at once, I shall arrange that immediately on my return home," he said.

"But the young people, will they wish it ?" Rachelle asked in dismay.

"Why Madame, you are truly becoming British in your outlook. Have you forgotten that in France young people are not consulted on this matter. Marriage is arranged for them, the older people know what is best, and our marriages turn out as well as the British ones, I am inclined to think."

Rachelle Durand thought that she and M. Furneaux were alone in the sitting-room, so they were, but in a small inside room used by M. Durand as a study, André was sitting. The door between the two rooms was ajar and André heard every word that was said. He escaped by another door at once, his head bowed low and his face white. He took his hat and went out feeling that he must be alone. Sorrow seeks solitude and at that moment André felt it would be torture to be with any human being. He went out into the street and paused for a moment longing for a quiet retreat. The cathedral of course promised seclusion, so he turned his steps thither, entered and in the dim light went into a pew and knelt down, burying his face in his hands.

His thoughts were in tumult. He had been feeling burdened ever since his father had pointed out to him that Leonie did not share his faith. But he had not deliberately faced the issue. Then another blow had come when he saw how eager Leonie was to go to France, but he had comforted himself with the thought "Absence makes the heart grow fonder." He had said to himself: "After a time I will seek her, she will be more likely to turn to me when she has had a taste of frivolity and wearied of it."

Now the final crushing blow had fallen. Leonie was to be married out of hand, no thought to be given to his claim. For a time as he knelt there he could only murmur: "Leonie, my little Leonie."

Then he began to realise that he was putting Leonie in the place of his Saviour and Master. It seemed to him as he knelt there that a Voice sounded in his heart: "Lovest thou Me ?"

André whispered: "Lord Thou knowest that I love Thee."

"Lovest thou Me more than any other ?" the Voice asked.

André thought, and a vision of Calvary came to him, of the One Who had suffered there for him and sincerely from his heart he was able to say: "Saviour, I love Thee best of all."

Peace came at length and André was able to leave the

building with a calm face and a serene mind. He was surprised when he came into the street to find that daylight had faded; it was now dusk, and when he had entered the cathedral it was high day.

The day came at last for Leonie's departure. André sought her early in the morning, he could not say his farewell with all the others, he had decided that he would be missing at that last moment.

He took her hand in his and said: " Good-bye little one. Don't forget if ever you want a friend, I shall be ready to help you."

" Oh André, you do look grave. Aren't you pleased that I have found my father and that I am going to have a gay time in my own home ? Are you cross ? Don't you think I ought to go ? "

Leonie pouted. André had always been her willing slave and his approbation was dear to her.

" Not cross dear, only sad. I wonder if you will find gaiety satisfying. Don't forget all you have learnt here of the Saviour. Your mother loved and suffered for Him. Oh, Leonie choose the highest."

Leonie pulled away her hand.

" You might say something kind and nice André, when I'm going away."

André forced a smile. " Of course I will Leonie. I wish you the best. Let us part friends. I shall never forget you, dear."

Leonie would have flung her arms around him as she had done many times, but André put her gently from him and stooping kissed her hand.

" Good-bye dear. Remember what I said, if ever you want a friend you will find me the same as ever."

He turned and went and Leonie's face was shadowed for a moment, but she was soon smiling again.

There were several little last things to do, and breakfast to have before her father and Henri would call for her. Aunt Marie, Lawrence and Lovedy came to see her off and Leonie felt a good deal pleased at being the most important person in the household and the centre of attraction. She went to put on her bonnet and cloak, Madame Durand and Ninon waiting on her and soon she was ready.

" Here they are," Ninon said as she looked out of the window.

All was bustle. M. Furneaux was flurried and excited. There was no time to waste, he declared. Leonie greeted them gaily, but when Madame Durand folded her in her arms the tears came and she clung to the one who had been so good to her.

" Oh mother, mother. I shall miss you," she said brokenly. " You will go on loving me, won't you ? "

" Always darling you can be sure of that, and I shall never cease to pray for you. God keep you and protect you, my darling."

M. Furneaux took Leonie's hand saying: " Come along my child, we must be off."

So with hasty kisses from them all, Leonie was led away.

The little group in the doorway stood watching and at the bend of the road, Leonie hung her head out of the coach window, and waved.

The tears had been hastily wiped away and once again Leonie was dimpling with smiles.

" Poor child," Rachelle Durand said with a sigh as she closed the door.

" We shall miss our little sunbeam, bonny, little Leonie," Gaston remarked and he asked: " Where is André ? I should have thought he would have been here to see her go."

Rachelle made no reply but she understood her son's absence.

Meanwhile Lawrence and Ninon were making the

most of this unusual meeting in the morning. They were very much in love with one another and both showed it in their happy faces.

Anyone who had not seen Lawrence since his boyhood days would not have recognised the sunny looking youth as he was now. Kindness had transfigured him. Ninon too had improved immensely. She would never be as pretty as Leonie, but there was gracious personality shown in all that she did, and there were many who thought Lawrence a fortunate man to have won so amiable a girl.

CHAPTER XXXV

LEONIE'S HOME

LEONIE enjoyed the journey immensely. She was eager for every new sight, and her father being in a good mood at the discovery of his daughter, who he had mourned as dead, and finding her so pretty and attractive, petted her.

Henri, she thought, seemed sullen and not inclined to wait on her as André had always done, and with her love of the approval of those about her, she set herself the task of winning Henri's regard. She could be exceedingly fascinating and M. Furneaux was amused at her wiles. He smiled to himself thinking: " I shall have no trouble with Leonie and when I make known my wishes to Henri, he will fall in with them, he has always been obedient. So all goes well."

What was lacking in Henri's attentions was amply supplied by old Jean, the manservant M. Furneaux had brought with him to England. He was at once Leonie's willing slave. He had been in the employ of M. Furneanx for many years, in fact from his boyhood. He had served Leonie's mother and for her sake he took Leonie under his special charge. He was able to tell her much about his lost mistress and Leonie loved to hear his tales. He also told her how greatly her father had changed since his wife's death. He had been devoted to her and her influence over him had been for good, without her he seemed to have lost his balance, naturally excitable he now gave way to fits of temper whenever his strong will was crossed. It seemed that because of his deep affection for his wife, it hurt him to talk of her, but Jean never wearied of speaking of his mistress.

Leonie asked him one day: "Could you not have saved her from her persecutors and kept me from wandering?"

"Alas, Mademoiselle I was in Switzerland with your father! We had gone there to find a home in safety for you both. If I had been with her, I wonder, should I have suffered too? Should I have stood firm? Alas! Alas! I am a coward. I have yielded to my master's wishes and conformed to the rules of the king. Mademoiselle—the old man lowered his voice—"I am a Huguenot at heart, but I have denied my Lord."

Leonie tried to comfort him. She said words she had often heard from the Durands and at the Huguenot services. "The Lord looketh on the heart."

"Ah yes Mademoiselle, but His Word also says: 'By Him actions are weighed.'"

Their conversation ended there for the moment. M. Furneaux came to claim Leonie's attention, he desired her company.

When at last they reached home, Leonie was delighted. The immense building, the beautiful grounds, the group of servants, made her heart swell with pride.

"I always thought I belonged to the aristocracy," she said to her father. "Ninon had such bourgeoisie ideas and the Giles family were . . . ." she paused for a word —"were so British. I felt different somehow."

M. Furneaux laughed heartily. "Of course you did my dear, birth tells. Now one day we must present you at Court, but there is no great hurry for that. I have many plans for you and I must see them accomplished."

Things went well from Leonie's point of view for a short time, neighbours called and Leonie was made much of by them all. Flattery, which was as nectar to her soul, was not wanting and Leonie heartily enjoyed every moment of her life.

A month had passed in the chateau, when one morning M. Furneaux called Leonie into his private room. It was a sombre looking apartment with many cupboards, a few books and some piles of documents on a desk. The chairs were hard and there were no cushions, a room meant for business and not comfort.

Leonie shivered with a sense of fore-boding.

" Sit down my dear. It is time I had a talk with you on one or two important matters. I have delayed this conversation because I wanted you to feel perfectly at home and accustomed to your surroundings ere I spoke. You are happy here ? "

" Oh yes, father. I love the place and you are so kind. Everybody seems pleased to have me here."

" That's right. I want you to be happy, my child. Now it is time you joined our church. There is no safety for any one in this land who belongs to any other religion."

" Your church ? " Leonie said wonderingly.

" Yes, yes. Do you not understand ? I have arranged that you shall accompany Henri and myself to mass on Sunday morning."

" But father, I am a Protestant."

" Nonsense my dear. Of course you were in England, for those good people who were so kind to you, were Protestants and young folk must be what their parents or guardians are. Now you must do what I wish."

" But father, my mother was a Protestant."

M. Furneaux winced. Leonie had touched on a sore spot.

He spoke grimly. " Yes and she paid dearly for it. It is because I wish to save you from a like fate that I insist on your joining the church of the land. I was obliged to do so, and so was Henri. I was not made for a martyr. It may be my faith was only of the head and not of the heart. True I honour those who, like your mother, stood fast, but I can see it is not in you any more than it was in me. We need discuss that no farther. You will go with me to mass on Sunday, before then Father Ambrose will be here to receive your confession. He will deal gently with you for he knows all about you and the influence you have been under."

Leonie's eyes grew big with fear and her father saw her fright. He patted her hand and said: "You need not be afraid, dear. Just do what you are told and all will be well. Now I have something more pleasant to tell you. You know Henri is my adopted son and not knowing that I had a daughter living, I have brought him up to believe himself my heir, I have made my will accordingly. Now I do not wish to alter that, instead I intend that Henri shall marry you. The betrothal will take place quite soon and then in a year from now you will be married. That will be fine, won't it? You will make a charming bride, my dear. Your jewels on that day will be worth a king's ransom. I must show them to you some day."

Leonie felt stunned for a moment or two as her father talked.

This had never occurred to her. She grew pale and then flushed.

"Father," she said tremulously, "Henri does not care for me."

"Well my dear, I look to you to make him. A woman can always do that, unless she is a fool. I have noticed you have tried to attract him, continue to do so, but in any case my mind is made up. I know what is best for you and for your future welfare. Now come and kiss me and smile. I don't like to see grave looks on my butterfly's face."

Leonie tried to obey, but her heart was heavy at the

thought of both the commands of her father. After the careful Protestant training the Durands had given her, she could not think lightly of taking the step on which her father insisted. The thought of confession and the mass filled her heart with dismay. But she had no intention of rebelling. Much as she disliked it, she must obey. And then to her surprise she found herself longing for André and contrasting him with Henri. André was so kind, so gentle and yet so strong, she had never realised how much he had meant to her until now when she was separated from him and being thrust into a marriage for which she had no desire.

But M. Furneaux's words were law to both the young people and he hastened to prepare for the betrothal. Meanwhile Leonie had to submit to making her confession and going to mass. She had no strength to resist, for she knew not the One Who can alone make strong and Who would have enabled her to refuse the wrong and stand for the right. She hated yielding and did so with a bad grace. Father Ambrose noted this and determined presently to take her in hand and break her proud spirit, but he was content at the moment to bide his time for so doing.

A few days before the time fixed for the ceremony of the betrothal, Leonie made one great effort to get her father to change his mind. She sought him when alone and said: "Father, I am sure Henri does not like me. Must you insist on this betrothal?"

Her lips trembled as she spoke for she was beginning to be somewhat afraid of her father.

She had indeed good cause for thinking Henri did not like her. He was bad tempered and positively rude to her whenever M. Furneaux was absent. Leonie guessed, and guessed rightly, that it gave Henri no pleasure that she had been found by her father. Before that, his position had been assured, now he felt unless he complied with M. Furneaux's desires he might find himself disinherited. The circumstances were developing a side of Henri's character hitherto unrevealed. He could be both selfish and cruel, while love of money and pride of place predominated in his nature. Leonie realised this, while her father was blissfully ignorant of it.

M. Furneaux looked at his daughter sternly.

" Do not let me hear any more of this nonsense. You know everything is settled. The guests are invited and all our neighbours are charmed about it. Several have said to me what a happy arrangement it is."

" And what if I refuse ? " Leonie said spiritedly. She repented the next minute for her father's rage was terrible. Accustomed to the gentle rule of the Durands, she was frightened indeed.

M. Furneaux raved at her, threatening the most awful penalties if she said another word. Trembling she fled from his presence, and dreaded meeting him again, but when she did he seemed to have forgotten, or had decided to ignore the scene, and petted her and spoke with great kindness.

Then came the ceremony of the betrothal. Many neighbours and friends were invited. The old château was crowded with guests, everybody seemed gay, save the two principal actors in the scene. To M. Furneaux's dismay they were gloomy. He again grew angry and scolded them heartily.

Leonie had to bear a torrent of stormy words and she was cowed.

" You ungrateful girl," her father said. " Have I not loaded you with gifts, fine clothes, jewels ? Am I not providing you with a husband ? Now understand, if you do not smile and behave prettily I shall find some way of punishing you when our guests have departed. Now no tears, you will spoil your looks."

He as suddenly relented as he had blazed up.

"Come and kiss me, my pet. There, there, be good. You must trust me that I know best."

Then he sought Henri and pointed out that unless the lad pleased him, he could easily make a new will and leave everything to Leonie.

So the two young people had to assume an air of gaiety they were far from feeling, and M. Furneaux not seeing below the surface, considered he had obtained his objective.

CHAPTER XXXVI

THE DISCOVERY

A FEW weeks passed uneventfully. Leonie grew more and more burdened as time went on. The gay doings paled, she could not get accustomed to the atmosphere of her father's house. He too, made things difficult, he was so changeable, sometimes scolding, sometimes petting, she longed for the calm peace and happiness of the old home. The older people Leonie had known had been so dependable, she had never known that anyone could be so erratic as her father. She grew frightened and timid, and with the addition of Henri's rudeness, she felt as though the pathway of life had changed from solid rock to shifting, treacherous sand.

Leonie was not the type of girl who could stand alone; she was like a sensitive plant blooming and flourishing in sunshine, but fading at the slightest blast of tempest. But in spite of this, the adverse circumstances were doing much to develop a naturally weak character. Leonie would be all the better for her experience.

The one person who was any comfort to her at this time, was old Jean. He accompanied her on her daily rides whenever her father could not, and Henri would not do so. Leonie welcomed these occasions. She learnt much about her mother, for Jean loved to talk of her and Leonie delighted in hearing stories of the mother she could not remember. It was the one gleam of sunshine in her life. In her turn she told Jean of the life and friends in Canterbury and when she spoke of André there was a quality in her tone which made the old man shake his head sorrowfully.

"Ah," he said to himself "that's the man my little Mademoiselle ought to marry. Things are alas ! tangled, but I can send up a prayer to God for her. He alone can help the poor young lady. As for M. Henri, we all know Mademoiselle Dorothée la Trobe is the one he loves. I wish indeed master was not set on his own way. 'Tis sad to see the young ones suffer."

One day Leonie and her father were seated in the salon. M. Furneaux had been talking of the wedding which was to take place in three months time, nine months having elapsed since the betrothal.

Everyone, save M. Furneaux could see how opposed Henri was to the marriage, but Henri managed to show a superficial interest in, and politeness to Leonie in M. Furneaux's presence. Poor lad, he was as miserable as Leonie, for he knew if he did not comply with his adopted father's wishes, he would be cut off without a penny. Brought up as he had been to a life of idleness and luxury what could he do ? To earn a living was impossible for him, or so he thought.

Oh ! how he regretted ever having wished his father to take him to England, if only they had remained in their own land, Leonie would never had been found and he could have married Dorothée.

The salon in which M. Furneaux and Leonie were seated was plentifully supplied with mirrors. There was one immediately opposite the door, which door stood open as the day was sultry, and this mirror reflected the long corridor which led to the door of the salon.

M. Furneaux suddenly asked Leonie: "Where is Henri ? I have not seen him since lunch, have you ?"

"I saw him a short time ago when I looked out of the window. He was walking in the pleasance with Dorothée la Trobe," Leonie replied.

M. Furneaux frowned. Then he said lightly: "They have been friends since childhood, like brother and sister.

Dorothée's father is, I understand, arranging a marriage for her with her cousin who lives in Paris."

He stopped suddenly. He was sitting where he had a good view of the mirror which reflected the corridor, Leonie sitting close to him.

Both were silent as they saw Henri and Dorothée come up the stairs and along the corridor. Their footsteps made no sound on the heavy velvet pile carpet. As they came along hand in hand, Henri suddenly paused and taking Dorothée into his arms kissed her passionately, over and over again, while Dorothée returned his embrace with evident fervour.

Leonie gasped. Would her father explode? She watched him anxiously. His face grew crimson, but he controlled himself, being too much of a gentleman to give way to passion before his young neighbour.

Henri and Dorothée entered. Henri exclaiming: "I had no idea you were here, sir. I brought Dorothée to see that new piece of tapestry you had hung yesterday."

Neither Henri nor Dorothée had any thought that they had been seen, but Dorothée somehow felt uncomfortable, the atmosphere seemed charged with an unpleasantness and constraint. M. Furneaux was coldly polite and Dorothée soon took her leave, Henri accompanying her to the door. No sooner had she departed than Jean sought him with a message from M. Furneaux desiring his presence at once.

Directly Henri entered the room, M. Furneaux gave rein to his annoyance. He stormed and scolded. Leonie burst into tears and trembled. Henri however was cool, he had no opportunity of speaking for M. Furneaux's anger was terrible.

He shouted: "You unscrupulous scoundrel, you little thought you could be seen in the mirror. I'll disown you, you ungrateful rascal. You shall leave this château today. Have I not cared for you from childhood, lavished gifts on you, given you every advantage and now you flout my wishes and make love to this girl while all the time you are affianced to my daughter."

He grew purple in the face and almost choked with rage.

Henri tried to get in a word to defend himself. "Leonie is being forced upon me I don't want her. I—I . . ."

He stopped for M. Furneaux stuttered, clutched at his throat and fell unconscious on the floor.

Henri rushed for Jean. The servants gathered and exclaimed with horror. Jean hurried a groom off for the physician. M. Furneaux was carried to his bed. When the physician arrived he pronounced it to be apoplexy and bled the poor sufferer, but all his efforts were unavailing. At midnight M. Furneaux passed away.

Poor Leonie suffered much from shock and could only remain in her room weak and helpless. Indeed she had no desire to leave it, she did not want to meet Henri. At first she did nothing but cry, but after a time grew calmer and as she rested on her couch she remembered some words from a Psalm she had learnt in childhood.

"Call upon Me in the day of trouble and I will deliver thee."

"This is indeed a day of trouble," she thought. "but can I ask God to help me? I have been so wrong, so careless. I have never sought God in my days of happiness, I have been so false, going to confession and mass, when all the time I knew how wrong it was. Dare I now seek God and ask His help? But oh I must, I must, I cannot face things alone."

She rose from her couch and for the first time in her life really prayed, brokenly she asked God to deliver her, that was all just then.

As she got up from her knees, her heart was filled with longing for her friends in England. Would she be able to go back to them ? She pondered as to what she could do. She supposed it would be as Henri said, but one thing she was quite determined about, she would not marry him. She next thought of her father's wealth, was it hers or would it belong to Henri ? M. Furneaux had talked freely to her and told her that years ago he made a will leaving everything to Henri, thinking his daughter was dead, but she knew that recently he had had visits from his lawyer, and she had once heard him say Henri had better be careful how he behaved, or he would find Leonie was in possession of all.

Henri had not been near her since her father's death two days ago, and she dreaded meeting him and she also feared seeing Father Ambrose for lately he had been very stern with her. Now she felt she would be at the mercy of these two men.

Chapter XXXVII

HER MOTHER'S JEWELS

LEONIE got tired of staying in her room, she felt restless and would like to have gone into the grounds, but she knew etiquette forbade her leaving the house until the funeral was over which was to take place the next day. So she wandered disconsolately from room to room, until she came to the little boudoir that had been her mother's favourite room. Leonie had often visited this apartment, she liked to sit on the tapestry covered chair by her mother's desk and try to visualise her mother. Everything had been left as it had been in the olden days and Leonie had many times examined the pictures and ornaments and looked into the desk.

To-day she once again opened the desk and fingered the papers scarcely knowing what she was doing. She moved a packet of letters and the light fell on a tiny brass plate she had not noticed before. She put her finger on it and as she did so she touched a spring, which sprang back and revealed a drawer at the back of the desk.

Leonie pulled it open and there inside lay a book, she took it out and exclaimed in surprise. "Why it is a Testament, my mother's."

She sat down at once by the window and turned the leaves, aimlessly at first, then her interest was roused by a chapter in the Acts of the Apostles. Her eye fell on a verse: "They knew Him not nor yet the voice of the prophets which are read every Sabbath day" (Acts 13: 27).

"That describes me. I have heard the Bible read every week, no, more than that, every day and yet I have not learnt to know Christ."

She read the context of the verse and shivered as she saw what ignorance of God and His message had led these people to do, they had condemned and crucified Christ, and for herself she realised that her indifference had led her to ignore the Saviour. She had known the Gospel in her head from childhood days, but had never felt her need of the Saviour. Now, it was as Madame Durand had thought it would be, sorrow had brought Leonie to seek Christ. She knelt once again, here, where her mother had so often prayed for her little daughter, here, on the same spot Leonie confessed her hardness of heart, her sins of vanity and selfishness and sought pardon.

When she rose from her knees, there was a serene look on her face, for she knew for the first time a peace of heart and a strength which made her feel she could face whatever was coming.

Would it be persecution ? She knew she could not go to mass on the next Sunday and Father Ambrose would want to know the reason.

To-day was Tuesday and she would have four days to pray for help and guidance.

The next day was extremely painful. Her father was buried with all the ritual of the Roman Catholic Church. Leonie remembered how Jean had told her that her father had been once a Huguenot and had seemed to possess a real knowledge of Christ as Saviour. Alas, fear had conquered in his heart, fear of persecution, of loss of this world's goods and now he had lost his soul. The words came to Leonie's mind: "What shall it profit a man if he gain the whole world and lose his own soul ?"

Her tears flowed at the thought.

When they returned to the house Leonie slipped away to her room but she was not allowed to stay there long. A messenger came saying she was needed in the salon. She would fain have excused herself, but feared that Henri would be annoyed, so she went to the room. She found her father's lawyer was about to read the will. The lawyer, an elderly man, placed a chair for Leonie and greeted her with a note of sympathy in his tone.

Leonie listened only half heartedly to the long reading, the technical terms puzzled her and she failed to grasp their meaning. She noticed however that Henri looked pleased, his face changed from a grim sullenness to eagerness and then he flushed and his eyes sparkled. Leonie was quick witted and she at once thought: " Henri is pleased, the will must be in his favour."

When the lawyer finished he turned to Henri and said: " I suppose I must congratulate you, sir."

Then he spoke to Leonie. " You understand Mademoiselle that this will of your father's was made ten years ago, two years after your mother's death, at the time he understood that you were dead. Everything is left to your father's adopted son Henri. I hope this will not grieve you, as I understand you are affianced and will be married shortly."

The pleased look faded from Henri's face. He glanced at Leonie and was about to speak but Leonie was quicker. She rose to her feet took the engagement ring from her finger held it out to Henri saying: " We are not affianced now. Neither of us have any desire for the marriage."

The lawyer gasped. " But my dear young lady, do you realise that you are penniless ? "

Leonie winced at the naked truth. She sat down again and turned pale.

"What will you do Leonie?" Henri asked. "You know, I think, that I intend to marry Dorothée. You will not wish to remain here."

The lawyer spoke quickly.

"Sir you will no doubt wish to make some provision for Mademoiselle Leonie?"

Henri merely shrugged his shoulders and waited for Leonie's reply.

She did not answer for a moment. She had, just then, a vision of Madame Durand's gentle smile and seemed to hear her saying the words: "There will always be a welcome for you here."

The two men were waiting, both felt amazed at Leonie's calm face when she said quietly: "I shall return to my friends in England. I should like to start as soon as possible. If you will be so good as to provide me with an escort, Henri, and the funds."

"Jean can accompany you Leonie," Henri said quickly. "He is well accustomed to travelling."

Henri was delighted at the thought of getting rid of Leonie so easily, and Leonie was surprised at her own lightsomeness.

"I shall soon be with them," she said to herself.

Jean too, when he heard of the proposal was pleased.

He sought Leonie and assured her he would take care of her. Then he whispered: "And Mademoiselle perhaps in spite of my apostacy, I can be received into the fellowship of the Protestant Church, for I am truly repentant. How glad I shall be to end my days with true Christians."

"Oh Jean, then you mean to remain in England. That will be nice."

" Yes Mademoiselle, my master is dead. I am free tc choose. I have saved a good few louis d'ors, my wants are simple. I shall have sufficient."

" I am sure my friends will never let you want, Jean," Leonie said.

Later that day Henri came to Leonie and said: I am arranging for you to leave on Friday, Leonie. You can have the coach to take you to the coast. I have given Jean money to pay your way. Once in England your adopted parents can take care of you. I have no more responsibility."

He spoke in a hard, cold fashion and Leonie felt hurt, and still more so when he added: " Dorotheé is coming here this evening, I want her to look over the family jewels and if there are any she does not want, you can have them."

" My mother's jewels ! " Leonie said quietly.

" They were your mother's, they are mine now," Henri replied.

So Leonie was to have what Dorothée rejected. She felt it keenly but Dorothée was of a more generous nature than Henri. She said when the caskets were opened: " Now Leonie you choose. Take which you like best."

" But why ? " Henri asked. " They are legally mine Dorothée, it is only by our courtesy and kindness that Leonie gets any."

Leonie was about to flare up and tell Henri some wholesome truths, but suddenly some words came into her mind, words learned at Madame Durand's knee, learnt heedlessly at the time, but now coming as a precious reminder. " Ye have in Heaven a better and an enduring substance."

After all what did it matter if Dorothée had the jewels. She would value something in memory of her mother, but otherwise they seemed of little worth.

Dorothée shrugged her shoulders at Henri's remark and insisted on Leonie selecting what she pleased.

So Leonie took a long string of pearls.

Henri spoke crossly. "You've been careful to pick out the most valuable of the lot."

"I did not know that, I can choose something else."

But Dorothée told her to keep the pearls. She preferred the brighter jewels, the red rubies, the glittering diamonds, the elusively tinted opals and the green emeralds. So it was left at that.

CHAPTER XXXVIII

CANTERBURY AGAIN

RACHELLE DURAND sat alone. Her face was thoughtful, even a trifle sad. The house seemed so quiet now without the girls, Ninon's wedding having taken place a month before. Rachelle was happy as far as Ninon was concerned, for Lawrence Giles was trustworthy, and all she could desire in a husband for her daughter and her home being only three miles distant, visits were frequent.

Rachelle's thoughts turned to Leonie. Her heart was heavy whenever she thought of her adopted child.

"If only Leonie belonged to the Saviour," she thought. "I should feel at rest, but in her lightheartedness, adrift from our restraining influence, a stranger to the keeping power of God, I fear there is no folly into which she might not fall. Poor child. Am I to blame that she was not won for Christ in her early days?"

From her position in the window Rachelle could see André approaching the house. A smile passed over her face. What a joy he was to his parents, so stedfast, so good to them, and to all with whom he came in contact. The smile was followed by a sigh.

"I wish the dear lad could forget Leonie and find happiness with some worthy girl," she said to herself.

She recalled at least three of their acquaintances, either of which she would be pleased to welcome as a daughter-in-law. Lovedy Giles especially.

Presently André came into the room.

"Alone mother," he said stooping over her and kissing her brow.

" Yes dear, but busy with many thoughts and prayers."

" Ah I can guess your mind travelled to France and you wished you could get a peep at Leonie and see how she is faring."

" Yes, you are right, I was thinking of the dear girl. The house seems so quiet without my two, it makes me feel old. I was just wishing André you could bring me a nice daughter-in-law. She would get a warm welcome. There's Lovedy or Clare or . . . ."

André interrupted.

" No no, mother mine. I shall never marry. I have lost Leonie and there can never be any other for me. I expect she is married to Henri by now. Did not M. Furneaux say that he should have the wedding in a year. It is a year and three weeks since Leonie left us. I only wish we knew that Henri is kind to her. I did not feel I could trust him but perhaps that was jealousy on my part."

Rachelle Durand sighed. She knew it was useless to try to make André change his mind.

" Sometimes I still hope that Leonie will weary of the life and turn back to us. I pray so much for her and I have the confidence that she will yet be brought to realise her need and seek the Saviour. Then perhaps . . . ." Rachelle paused.

" But if she is married Mother, there will be no coming back to us, at any rate not as our little Leonie. I fear it is useless our indulging in day dreams. I feel however I could be content if I knew she was happy and had found salvation."

How little the two thought, as they sat talking, that their dear one was drawing near. At that very moment a carriage hired at the port was wending its way into Canterbury. Jean was seated on the box beside the coachman, Leonie was inside. She sat upright, her face tense with emotion. Sometimes she flushed, sometimes paled. Would she find all as she had left it. Would her adopted parents welcome her wholeheartedly. She remembered that both M. and Madame Durand could speak very gravely at times and Leonie felt if they lectured her she could only admit that she deserved it. She had left them so heartlessly, scarcely acknowledging her indebtness to them, barely a word of thanks for all the kindness she had received from them.

And André would he have changed? Perhaps André had forgotten her and found someone to love who would requite his affection and be more worthy of him than herself. It was a new and humble Leonie that was returning to them.

Leonie's heart thumped uncomfortably as the horses turned into the familiar street and drew up at the door.

Jean got down from the box as quickly as his stiff old limbs would permit, and would have handed Leonie out with polite ceremony, but she had already alighted and was knocking at the door, impatient for it to open and yet trembling with excitement and apprehension.

It was Betsy the maid who opened it and exclaimed: " La if it isn't Mistress Leonie, or is it your ghost? You look white enough and I had a dream last night."

But Leonie did not stay to listen, she hurried past the girl saying: " Where is Madame ? "

" In the kitchen, she's just come downstairs," Betsy answered.

Leonie flung open the kitchen door. Rachelle Durand had just immersed her hands in a basin of flour, she turned to the door wondering who was making this impetuous entrance and then she cried: " Leonie, Leonie, my child."

" Oh Mother, Mother! " was all Leonie could say, as she hid her face on Madame Durand's breast.

Betsy had run to the work room, where André now was, and beckoned mysteriously to him. He came to see what it was she wanted.

" Master André, she's here. She's in the kitchen " was all Betsy said.

André's thoughts immediately flew to Leonie, but he checked himself. Of course Betsy only meant Ninon. The girl was given to excitement on small provocation. However he followed her to the kitchen and to his utter amazement he found that the impulse of his mind had not been at fault. Leonie was there. His first thought was one of staggering joy. But then he remembered Henri and after greeting Leonie, he said: " And where is your husband? Did he bring you here? "

" André, I have no husband. Henri did not want to marry me nor I him, I must tell you all about it."

But after all it was Jean who told the Durands the story, for the strain under which Leonie had passed had told on her health, and even as André was looking at her, she staggered and would have fallen if he had not caught her in his arms.

" Poor child," Madame Durand said. " She is exhausted. Bring her upstairs, André, I will get her to bed. We can hear all she has to tell us later.

Presently Rachelle decided to send for the physician, who, when he came said Leonie must be kept quiet for a time. No one was to see her but Madame Durand. André chafed at this, but his mother assured him it would be only a day or two before he could talk to Leonie.

André consoled himself by taking the opportunity of having much conversation with Jean, whom Madame Durand welcomed for Leonie's sake.

From him André learnt of M. Furneaux's death; of Henri's love for Mademoiselle Dorothée la Trobe; of Leonie's conversion and of M. Furneaux's will.

The story of Leonie's conversion was the bit of news that caused André, his father and mother great rejoicing.

André felt the last barrier between him and Leonie was removed, if she returned his love, and somehow André felt hopeful about this. From the wistful eagerness of her face when André greeted her in the kitchen, he took courage, believing he was about to have the desire of his heart, after this long delay.

He was impatient to make sure. His mother laughed at him and said Leonie must not be excited. However when his face fell she was all sympathy: "Don't worry dear. I think I can assure you from the conversation I have had with Leonie, that all will be well."

And with this André had to be content.

It was three days later when Madame Durand gave her consent to Leonie dressing and coming down to the sitting-room. It was evening and twilight, André was seated alone, thinking of Leonie, but with no idea that she was up and about. Presently he felt a slight touch on his shoulder and there she stood, dressed in a white gown, looking pale and shadowy in the dim light.

No words were needed. André had planned to say much. Leonie had thought she would ask him to forgive her for all her selfish, hardhearted ways in the past, but none of this was said just then. Instead André held out his arms and Leonie yielded to his embrace.

Love gave them both a perfect sense of unity. André was rewarded for his long years of faithful waiting. Leonie had learnt much, and would make him a far better wife for her experience of suffering than she would have done had she never traversed that rough bit of road.